HE

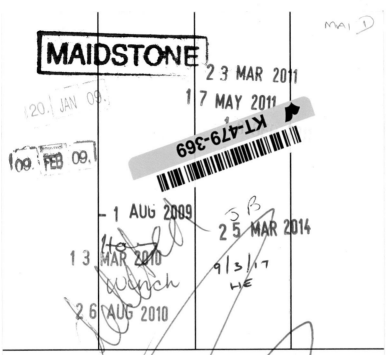

MAI D

Please return on or before the latest date above.
You can renew online at *www.kent.gov.uk/libs*
or by telephone 08458 247 200

CUSTOMER SERVICE EXCELLENCE

Libraries & Archives

00884\DTP\RN\07.07   LIB 7

TRIPLE CROSS
AT TRINIDAD

L. L. FOREMAN

WHEELER
CHIVERS

This Large Print edition is published by Wheeler Publishing, Waterville, Maine, USA and by BBC Audiobooks Ltd, Bath, England.
Wheeler Publishing, a part of Gale, Cengage Learning.
Copyright © 1971 by Leonard London Foreman.
The moral right of the author has been asserted.

LIBRARY OF CONGRESS CATALOGING-IN-PUBLICATION DATA

Foreman, L. L. (Leonard London), 1901–
    Triple cross at Trinidad / by L.L. Foreman. — Large print ed.
        p. cm.
    ISBN-13: 978-1-59722-696-7 (softcover : alk. paper)
    ISBN-10: 1-59722-696-3 (softcover : alk. paper)
    1. Large type books. I. Title.
PS3511.O427T75 2008
813'.54—dc22   2007044813

BRITISH LIBRARY CATALOGUING-IN-PUBLICATION DATA AVAILABLE

Published in 2008 in the U.S. by arrangement with
Golden West Literary Agency.
Published in 2008 in the U.K. by arrangement with
Golden West Literary Agency.

U.K. Hardcover: 978 1 405 64418 1 (Chivers Large Print)
U.K. Softcover: 978 1 405 64419 8 (Camden Large Print)

Printed in the United States of America
1 2 3 4 5 6 7 12 11 10 09 08

TRIPLE CROSS
AT TRINIDAD

1

The black horse pricked its ears and snorted, but kept to a steady pace, entering the town from the south. It was a long-legged, powerful animal, with a wickedly aggressive nature, so the snort didn't stem from complaint.

"I agree with you," murmured its rider aloud, in the habit of a man who, living much alone, took his horse into his confidence at times. "Something's wrong here."

He was big-boned, a large man whose way of life required a dependable mount with good sense and uncommon stamina as well as a fast turn of speed when called for. He sent a gray stare ranging for evidence of trouble. None was visible. Everything was quiet here at the south edge of town.

The quietness itself struck him as false, like the leaden stillness of air that presaged a thunderstorm. His horse sensed it.

Serenely blue, cloudless from horizon to

horizon, the sky shone innocent of any threat of storm. The threat, then, if it actually existed — if his senses weren't untrue — stemmed from lurking men somewhere close ahead of him.

"Laying for me?" he muttered. The black horse paced sedately into a street leading up to the plaza, the center of town where noise promised liveliness.

He shook his head slightly to his own question. It was scarcely possible that enemies, of whom he had many, could have raced ahead to bushwhack him here. Never had he dropped a hint to anyone of where he was going. He trusted nobody: first rule of a long rider. Even a friend might let loose an unguarded word. Vigilant care was the price he paid for staying alive in a reasonably healthy condition, and he rarely fell delinquent in the bill.

Coming up from New Mexico, crossing into Colorado, he had expected to find this town of Trinidad roaring full blast and bursting at the seams with a glorious boom of prosperity. A pleasurable anticipation. Cash flowing fast, high-stakes poker, free-and-easy law. That suited him, he being the kind of man he was.

Trinidad swaggered this year in its prideful prestige as a brand-new cattle capital, a shipping center for market herds from New Mexico, Arizona, West Texas. Trinidad had been reached by the iron tracks of the Atchison, Topeka & Santa Fe Railroad, the A.T.&S.F., which was building toward Santa Fe — old Santa Fe slumbering in the sun in the heart of New Mexico, Land of Poco Tiempo, the country where time didn't matter, hadn't mattered for for three centuries since the Spanish men-at-arms clanked in looking for gold.

The railroad never touched Santa Fe. It bypassed the ancient city by sixteen miles, because of steep grades. But it did reach Trinidad on the Santa Fe Trail, on the northeast, eventually, and there the engineers paused to ponder on the difficulties of Raton Pass — a road that had wrecked many a trader's wagon in past days.

Trinidad then wakened to the fact that it was a railhead town. It formed a junction, connecting the railroad with the northbound cattle trails — the old Trinidad Trail, for only one, from the Llano River, way south, best cattle country of Texas. The cowmen and cattle dealers wanted a shipping point. Trinidad was it. To hell with Abilene and Dodge City. Trinidad was nearer, this year, until the railroad pushed on past it.

Trinidad was having its shining hour

9

forced on it, along with the inevitable side issues of overnight wealth. The shark gamblers and Lulu girls, the gunmen, the pickpockets and rollers.

None of those things accounted for the hush that met the big man at this south end of town. The virtues of temperate soft-footing, if any, had never yet gone hand-in-hand with cattle prosperity.

With the hard wisdom of experience he searched again for symptoms. Nothing. The hour was sliding into evening dusk, yet no lights studded the small windows along here. The only visible life in the street was a shabby young man smoking the butt of a brown cigarette, squatting on his heels. A busted trail hand, from his looks, left derelict after blowing in his pay. Every railhead town always had a residue of recklessly improvident young tramps.

Explosive events ambushed in the unnatural stillness, the big man felt. This section of town wasn't any different from the rest. A section composed of shacks, cribs, gambling saloons where far-from-home cowmen could get a fast whirl at anything they desired, for a price. But it stayed silent.

"Me?" he mused again. His ways were haunted by enemies, violence, sudden emergencies.

its very name was Spanish: Trinity, commemorating the union of Father, Son, and Holy Ghost. In the same religious spirit they named the vast, overshadowing mountains westward the Sangre de Cristos — Blood of Christ — the mountains which did indeed glow red as the sun sank, and would forever.

Being either clannish or less affluent, the Mexican people of Trinidad supported only one saloon of their own, called the Casa Colorado, so its sign said — a name that could have meant simply the Red House. It was painted red. It jutted its front right out to the edge of the boardwalk, onto the street, and there the boardwalk ended.

The big man took in his surroundings with a sweeping look. He drew his dark eyebrows down, annoyed at the shabby saddle tramp who still kept pace alongside him.

"*Vamose,* bum!"

"I'm not a bum, any more'n you are! I —"

"Don't tell me your troubles!"

At this end of the main street a door banged shut. For a minute that was the only sound. The black's rider became aware that he and the tramp hadn't left the solemn hush behind. It had followed their course to the heart of town, and now it surrounded

13

them like a spreading blight, extinguishing lights in the dusk and smothering all the common noises. The black horse snorted again.

"Back there," said the tramp, "three fellers in that little Mexican livery were set to get me. They had me where I couldn't either move in or slide off. They —"

"So you used me for cover!"

"I was about to apologize for it, Mr. Bishop."

"Save your breath!" Annoyed, the big man didn't ask how he came to know his name. His restless life made him known to many people with whom he hadn't any personal acquaintance. Too many.

"My name's Ballinger. I'm called Banjo Ballinger down in Arizona, account I own the Banjo brand. Near Buckeye, my place. You ever in Buckeye? Good town."

Bishop didn't even grunt acknowledgment. There were few towns left, throughout the Southwest and the border states of Old Mexico, where he could go without somebody recognizing him. All too few. He remembered Buckeye, vaguely. A lousy town, to his viewpoint. Tight. He wasn't letting any busted young Buckeye cowman cozy up to him. He doubted if Ballinger owned anything more than his gun and wornout garb.

"I saw you once in Tucson years ago, Mr. Bishop, in a gambling house. You tipped a skinny youngster twenty dollars for fetching you a plate of grub. Me."

"I probably did it for luck. *My* luck."

"I played the roulette wheel with it, on a hunch, betting on black, and ran it up to more'n a thousand before they threw me out. It later gave me my start in cows. Luck stayed with me right along," Ballinger said. "I prospered."

"Not now, from your looks!" commented Bishop.

"It took a bad turn since I came here," Ballinger conceded. "Trinidad's been mighty tough on me."

Five men filed out from Doc Sunday's Livery Stable, and, stepping lightly, formed abreast, blocking the runway. The force of the solemn hush had its focal point then, in their faces, eyes, their position of drawing a deadline.

Ballinger shoved his hat back, the action watched closely by the five waiting men. "The word's gone out to stop me from getting hold of a horse," he said. "Doc Sunday would loan me one if they'd let him. Could we bust these guys?"

The cool assumption of partnership

brought a scowl. "Damn your gall, don't try using me any more'n you've already done!" Bishop answered harshly. "It's your problem, not mine!" Hard to the bone, a twenty-dollar tip casually given and forgotten years ago meant nothing to him. He certainly wouldn't encourage a personal tie to be built on it, especially by an impoverished pilgrim who evidently had brought trouble on himself.

His horse was Bishop's first concern, and the livery was his objective. He didn't believe at first that the mute challenge of the five men was aimed at him as well as at Ballinger, who paused on the opposite boardwalk to roll a cigarette, seeming to spend all his attention on it. Only when he drew up to them, and they stood fast, did Bishop realize that he was included, that Ballinger had actually succeeded in making it appear that he was an ally.

"Kindly make way," he requested, none of his anger sounding in his moderate tone. The anger was for Ballinger.

They eyed him consideringly, not quite sure what to make of a man whose large presence weighed strongly upon them, yet who spoke mildly. He was an enigma to those who hadn't been around enough to recognize rare signs.

His single-breasted frock coat of black broadcloth, with white shirt and string tie, hinted of the clergy — Calvinist, or something else as remote from frivolity, austerely funereal. The erect bearing of his tall body demanded respect. His black hat, flat-crowned, should have heightened the ministerial impression. It didn't. It contradicted the whole effect, by the rakish sweep of its broad brim; a go-to-hell slant.

Under the shading brim, a strong-lined face, worldly wise and saturnine, dispelled all suggestion of divinity. Its forbidding chill made the puritanical garb an appropriate part of the man.

It was his face that caught and held the disturbed regard of the five deadliners barring the runway into Doc Sunday's Livery Stable. In their limited fashion they, rangeland gunmen, could read character. Here was character for anyone to read.

The nose of the big man was a predatory beak, a bit dented by past brawls. The deep-set gray eyes were startling against the darkly sun-browned skin; they looked as if they'd shine in the dark, or glare, icily ruthless. The wide mouth, hard yet oddly generous, tolerant, was stamped with a sardonic quirk of humor.

A dominant and dangerous hawk of a

man, this, not one to swallow any insult to him. One of a vanishing breed, a dwindling fraternity of hardcased wanderers who, for good or bad, put their mark on the reaching Western frontiers. They died young, usually, by jungle law, shot down in some dusty street or chaparral fight. Or they got worn out and sank into obscurity, nerve gone.

This big, dark rider survived, his nerve very plainly unimpaired, calmly flaunting an arrogant self-confidence that had to be based on ability.

But the five men were committed to blocking the runway into the livery stable. They couldn't break their stand against him without bringing ridicule upon themselves, and loss of pride.

He understood that. He wasn't entirely uncharitable. Nor did he want trouble at the outset of his potential sojourn in Trinidad. Trouble had its inevitable place, after sessions at the card tables, when a poker shark tackled the problem of packing his winnings out of town. All in good time. Seeking a peaceful compromise, he repeated his mild request.

"Kindly make way." To it, he added, his tone hardening only slightly, "I want to put up my horse."

Again they misjudged moderateness. One

of them sidled out of line, opening a gap, drawling, "Go right ahead." He was bucktoothed and had a pointed chin, and his protruding eyes promised mischief, daring Bishop to pass through.

So it was that serious. Farewell to hopes of compromise. They were under orders, he surmised, from someone who thought he was here to help Ballinger. There was no other logical reason for their belligerence. That damned Arizona brushbuster had hooked him into his affair, whatever it was.

2

His move. The buck-toothed one had passed the deal to him. Bishop nudged his black horse forward and rode through onto the runway.

Across the street, Banjo Ballinger called quietly to him, "Watch out!"

The warning wasn't needed. Turning his head, Bishop had already caught the buck-toothed young badman in the act of taking a kick at the black to make it jump. He did three things swiftly and efficiently. He spun the black around, stirrup-booted the would-be kicker, and flipped out a gun from under his ministerial coat. The gun was heavy, long in the barrel. It roared a shot, but not at the buck-toothed one. That one lay gasping in the street, booted out of action.

A hat sailed off, a fine Stetson, punctured through both sides. Its owner, who had probably spent a month's pay on that costly headgear, turned and grabbed for it. A material mistake. Bishop's long leg rammed him where he wasn't looking and he skated face-down in the dirt until he fetched up against the edge of Doc Sunday's runway.

The heavy gun blared once more. Ballinger came running. Another of the five lost his hat, and crouched, raising empty hands in supplication to the shattering thunderbolt. With a swipe of his gun barrel Bishop buffaloed another, then laid a freezingly quizzical stare on the remaining two.

"I didn't buy chips in your game, but you dealt me in," he said, and now his tone was anything but mild. His stare dipped at their drawn guns. "Want to play it out?"

He knew their kind. Railhead toughs — all railheads spawned them. Young badmen, mostly still green from the range and spoiled by the garish life of a wide-open town. Cockerels ruffling in high feather, until a fighting game-cock swooped in.

They shook their heads numbly, dazed by the big man's sudden and devastating eruption of violence. He was before them, Ballinger behind them. They dropped their guns.

"Creest!" one mumbled. "That came quick!" It had all happened in less than half a minute.

Dark doorways spilled onlookers, apparently none of them would-be combatants against the big man, for he heard a voice among them say, "He sure took 'em!"

Lights came on in the Silver Spur, showing it to be a large establishment equipped with gambling tables, dance floor, a long bar visible through the windows. A man wearing a badge, and carrying a rifle, a Sharp's, emerged from the narrow office of the town marshal. A girl with a double-barreled shotgun raced on pattering feet past the marshal. She eluded nimbly the marshal's grasp at her, and came running on purposefully down the street.

Everything broke up then. The town marshal shouted at the girl, who ran on. Ballinger took the girl under his arm, running with her; he and she were evidently well acquainted. The town marshal halted, letting the muzzle of his Sharp's rifle hang low, signifying that he wasn't about to try using that weapon on anyone at present.

The flare-up was settled for the time being. Bishop went on into the livery barn, where he gave definite orders concerning the care of his horse, after the stableman lit the overhead lanterns. The stableman, impressed both by the man and the animal, vowed assurance of good service. Spying a tiny sand crack in the front right hoof, he offered to treat it. He paused, bobbing his head respectfully to a little man who came forward from the rear of the barn, where there was a double row of horse stalls.

"This crack, Doc . . ."

"I'll take care of it myself."

The little man spoke in the light and lisping voice of a child. His age-lined face was gentle, solemn. He wore a plug hat, carried an old leather satchel, and smelled of liniment. He smiled mistily at Bishop, then more clearly at the black, running his eyes knowledgeably over it.

"I'll take it as an honor, sir, to tend personally to this fine horse," he declared. "No charge. I saw what you did to Conant's hoodlums out there — a lesson they richly deserved!"

"You a vet?" Bishop inquired with a tinge of doubt. Veterinarians weren't usually small men, not this small at least.

"I am Elias P. Sunday, a full accredited practitioner of veterinary medicine and surgery. This is my, ah, domain." A fluttery hand waved around at the establishment. "As its owner and manager, I offer you freely its facilities. In all modesty, I'm equipped to deal with anything in my profession. Don't let my short size under-

23

rate your opinion of me."

"A man's as big as he's big inside."

"True! Men as big as you are, I've . . ."
Doc Sunday broke off. "A magnificent
horse, this!"

Bishop nodded agreement. "All right,
Doc, you take care of him. But give me the
bill. You're not in business for your health."

"Will you be staying long here in Trinidad?"

"Few days, maybe. Depends on *my* business."

When he came out of the livery, the street
appeared to be normal, no signs left of his
run-in with Conant's hoodlums — whoever
Conant was. Lights were on in the Silver
Spur, so he bent his course that way because
it was near and looked promising. He
passed by Ballinger, who stood in a doorway
talking with the girl of the shotgun — a
pretty girl, he noted. Returning Ballinger's
nod, Bishop went on to the saloon.

Like the town marshal, he wasn't inclined
to investigate the reasons for the flare-up.
Unlike that lawman, though, he simply
didn't care a damn what might have caused
it. Life was too spotted with such eruptions,
for a man to fritter away his time digging
into the roots of them. Anyway, right now
his inclinations ran in the direction of a

drink, a cigar, and some constructive poker, in that order.

He had a double bourbon and was lighting a long cigar, when the marshal entered the Silver Spur and came up to him at the end of the bar. They stood together, two large men exchanging weighing looks. The arrival and direct approach drew notice from the barroom crowd. Voices lowered.

The lawman gravely accepted the casual offer of a drink, aware that the offer was a test aimed toward discovering his present intentions. He waited until the bartender poured it and moved away.

"I'm Tom Conant," he introduced himself. "Town marshal." He gazed fixedly at the whiskey glass without touching it, masking his eyes by squinting them half shut. "I know who you are. You're Rogue Bishop."

Bishop took the cigar from his mouth, trimmed its end with strong white teeth, and said correctingly, "Rogate Bishop."

Only to a few, very few, did he permit the familiarity of calling him Rogue. The nickname was not of his own choosing, though it hadn't been cheaply earned. Gambler and gunfighter, free-lance troubleshooter on occasion when the stakes warranted it, he was a loner with a saturnine sense of dignity.

Marshal Tom Conant took the correction, making no comment, knowing from repute that Bishop, pushed, could be as bitingly devastating in speech and manner as in his actions. Bishop looked at him, then on farther at the card tables where poker chips were building up in interesting stacks.

"I rode a long way here." His deepset eyes chilled. "I wouldn't like you spoiling my visit."

Conant shook his head. "Not me. I know my limitations, and I've got a wife and daughter to think of. No, it won't be me, Bishop. It'll be Banjo Ballinger's enemies. They believe you came to Trinidad to troubleshoot for him."

"They're wrong."

"Try telling 'em that! Already it's all over town how you sided him and busted those five. And Ballinger acts like you're an old friend of his."

Bishop didn't bother to argue. This Tom Conant surely wasn't the one that Doc Sunday had meant when he spoke of "Conant's hoodlums." Not this middle-aged man with family cares and limited abilities, trying to keep some semblance of law and order in a roaring boomtown.

"Mind coming to my office?" Conant asked. "Just for a minute. I've got something private to say." He left his drink still untouched on the bar. "The games'll be higher when we get back. Town's loaded with cash nowadays."

"Okay, Marshal. A minute."

They left the saloon. Outside, pacing toward his office, the marshal grew confidential. "In this town the job of chief marshal is elective, like a sheriff's. My term expires soon. I'm running for re-election."

"Your past record's good, I hope," said Bishop.

"Not bad. But if you raise a real bust at this late time — if you damage some of the voting citizens — where does it put me? I'll have to come at you, or quit. And as I said before, I know my limitations. So I ask you —"

The marshal stopped midway up the street. His eyebrows bushed in a heavy frown having nothing to do with election problems. Slowly walking the shadows toward the plaza went two figures close together, Ballinger and the shotgun girl.

"Vada!" Conant rapped out. "Get back home, right now! Ballinger, stay away from my daughter! I'm warning you for the last time!" An urgent worry edged the command. There was more to this than the commonplace concern of a protective parent.

27

The pair broke apart reluctantly. Ballinger turned around, giving the impression of being on the verge of blasting a hot retort at Conant. Restrained by the presence of the girl, he tipped his hat to her, murmuring something. After an oddly surprised look at Bishop, he walked on alone. The girl blazed a rebellious stare at her father, then she cut off into a sidestreet.

"Vada's my only kid," Conant said in half apology to Bishop for the interruption. "She's a handful! What d'you do with a daughter when she grows up all of a sudden an' gets a mind of her own?"

Bishop didn't feel qualified to answer, not having met that particular problem personally in his free-roving life. He was on the outside, a predator rather than a participant. These honey-haired young girls with bosoms and warm eyes were a juicy enticement to marriage — if a man had that in mind — but he mistrusted the set of pretty Vada's determined little chin. A handful, yes, raising more disruption than a woolly lamb in a cowcamp.

"She's taken up with that feller, Banjo Ballinger. Him! Proddy Arizona rip!" Conant continued on toward his office. "As you know, Ballinger drove a herd up here —"

28

"I don't know!" Bishop cut in. "He's nothing to me!"

Conant twitched a shoulder, unconvinced. "All right. He sold his herd. Lost the money. Now he's trying every which-way to kick up hell about it. Dammit, I ain't responsible for his money! Trinidad's my bailiwick, an' he didn't lose it here!"

Bishop glanced up the street after the departing Banjo Ballinger. That busted young cowman would likely go a long way toward kicking up hell, until somebody killed him. He was full of fight and nerve. He'd had the cool gall to inveigle him — Bishop — into his tight spot, making it appear that he had a formidable backer, while in fact he stood alone.

"How much money did he lose, Marshal?"

"Forty thousand dollars."

"That's a sizable sum." Bishop gazed after Ballinger with heightened interest.

"There ain't a chance he'll ever recover it," Conant stated flatly. "Nor anybody else for him," he added.

"Meaning me!"

"No offense. A word of advice, is all."

As if he sensed that they were discussing him, Banjo Ballinger turned and looked back at them.

"He won't last long," Conant predicted.

"It's a wonder he's still alive. Bishop, you're a sharp man, I know. Too sharp to waste your time on cash that's gone beyond recall. You're a troubleshooter for profit. Believe me, there ain't a mite of profit for you in Ballinger!"

Holding his irritation in check, Bishop said, "That's not what I came to Trinidad for." But he realized that the words didn't bear any effect. The violent circumstances attending his arrival, coupled to his reputation, had stamped his visit here with a false significance.

Again a shrug of disbelief. "D'you still aim to stay a while?"

"For a few poker sessions, sure."

They stopped before the marshal's lighted office, and through the window Bishop saw the small, shabbily neat figure of Doc Sunday, steel-rimmed spectacles on his nose, reading a newspaper by the light of the lamp, his old leather satchel on the floor by his side. The veterinary and the town marshal were apparently cronies.

"Seeing I can't change your mind," said Conant, "I ask you a favor. Let me make you a deputy marshal."

"Why?"

"It'll help to clear me with the voting citizens, if things pop. I can say you acted on the side of the law, and they won't expect me then to stand up against you. Wait, I'll get you a badge. You don't need to wear it. Just have it handy, in case." Conant entered his office.

Bishop moved aside from the lighted window, more from habit than anything. He thought Conant's stratagem a bit comic, but he recognized the prudent motives and was tolerantly ready to co-operate. Public officeholders frequently had to pull devious tricks to hang onto their jobs. He bore no grudge against law officers, individually, as long as they didn't crowd him.

He heard Conant pull open a desk drawer and ransack through it for a spare deputy badge. Doc Sunday asked a question in his childish voice. The lamp was carried to the desk, closer to the window, and its light spread out widely on the boardwalk.

While he waited, Bishop surveyed the street. The Silver Spur Saloon had drawn much of the life of the town into it, while other establishments down the street didn't appear to be doing so well. The Casa Colorado, and a beer hall facing it, hadn't even lighted up yet. It struck him as a good town, though, a free-and-easy kind of town, untrammeled as yet by civic reformers and similar bluenose squelchers. He anticipated some bracing poker in the Silver Spur.

Conant came out of his office, flipping a badge from one hand to the other — a gesture that seemed curiously frivolous, out of keeping with his rather stolid nature. The bit of metal flashed shining in the light of the window.

"Here you are." He held it up.

Bishop had to step into the light to take it, frowning at the marshal, and slipped it into a pocket of his coat. Something rang untrue. It put him more than normally on his guard. He started to return to the Silver Spur.

Conant, backing into his office, called to him in an undertone, "Watch out, Bishop!"

The warning might have been meant in a general sense, rather than as a pressingly immediate alarm, but it set off instant reflex action in Bishop. He ducked and side-stepped, his hands slicing down under his coat in the same swift blur of movement. Within a few seconds he revised drastically his approval of Trinidad as a good town for pleasantly profitable poker. Trinidad was dynamite.

3

Everything broke at once. A gun down the street cracked at the spot that Bishop had vacated. It cracked again, fast, closely following his shift. A sharpshooter. The marshal's office went dark, a help to Bishop, its lighted window blacked out behind him. The Silver Spur's lamps blinked out next. Gunfire blared from the jutting red front of the Casa Colorado. Carbines, he judged by the sound. Firing blind at him. What in hell was all this about?

Running feet hit the boardwalk, approaching from up the street. Men could be heard spilling out of the Silver Spur by its alley side door, their intentions unknown. The street had abruptly become a wildly bullet-screaming ambuscade. No reason for it, as far as Bishop knew, unless the town had more than its share of flaming lunatics.

He leaped for the cover of the marshal's office. The lunatics were obviously out to

eliminate him. No poker this night. A sting-
ing punch high in the leg threw him off-
stride. His toe struck the raised doorstep.
He took a header into the marshal's office
and rammed the desk out of place.

"You an' your goddam deputy badge, Conant!" he swore, picking himself up. His
eyes glimmered dourly in the darkness. He
spat out the mashed remains of his cigar. "I
think you're a Jonah! Or a Judas! What
brought *that* on? You oughta know — you
squalled two seconds ahead of it!"

Conant's voice responded in a mutter, "I
had a hunch, just before the first shot. It
was Doc Sunday who blew out the lamp.
Doc?" There was no reply. "Guess he's gone
out the back door. Doc ain't much of a
hand to —"

A fresh burst of gunfire roared in the
street, this time from the direction of the
Silver Spur. The front window of the marshal's office dissolved, spraying glass slivers,
and Conant shouted commandingly, "Quit
that! I'm in here!"

A man came plunging through the open
doorway into the office. Whirling around,
flinging himself down, he hammered rapid
shots at the Silver Spur. Bishop, guns
cocked, changed his mind about quenching
the rashness of the uninvited newcomer.

"That you, Ballinger?"

"Sure!"

At Conant's shout the firing slackened, ceased, and a sullen hush settled over the darkened street. Backing in from the doorway, Ballinger got to his feet, commenting, "I knew that was due to bust!"

"You did, eh?" The edge of Bishop's temper sharpened. "Dammit, did you get a hunch too?" he rasped.

It angered him that he, main target of the gun storm, didn't know the why and wherefore of it. Others knew — Conant and Ballinger, obviously, and the sharpshooter and carbine-blazers in the Casa Colorado. And the Silver Spur crowd. But not him. It was exasperating. Furthermore, he had got tagged. A flesh wound in his leg. Nobody could take that liberty without paying for it. A matter of personal principle.

"No. More'n a hunch." Ballinger fed fresh shells into his gun, dropping empties on the floor. "Def'nate knowledge, sir." His tone altered, roughening. "Mr. Conant!"

"Well?"

"Your pistoleers just now made another try at me, as witness the busted window. They took advantage o' the Casa shooting. Your order, I don't doubt!"

"No, you brought it on y'self!" Conant

35

snapped. "You've stung 'em!"

"I've stung 'em again! You better call 'em off me!"

"I got no hold on their private fights."

"You're lying," Ballinger said without heat, stating it as a fact, a sorry fact that he regretted. "Mr. Bishop — the 'buscado in the street was aimed at you. Only you!"

"I know that." Bishop touched his punctured thigh. One more scar. "Why me?"

"There's a feller who doesn't like you, I reckon. In the Casa Colorado. Made you jump, didn't he?"

"He did!"

"What'll you do about him, Mr. Bishop?"

"Don't ask damfool questions!" Bishop felt his way in the dark to the rear door. "I'll call on him!" he said shortly. Meaning he was going for a kill. He'd had enough of mystery, of unexplained hostility. More than enough. Somebody had clipped him. He would clip that sharpshooter; then — only then — ask questions. One thing at a time.

"I'll come along." Ballinger followed him.

"I generally tend to my own business! I recommend you do the same!"

"That's what I'm doing. I've got some business to tend to with that feller in Casa Colorado, too, like you. Mine's money business. Forty thousand dollars."

"That," Bishop granted, "buys you in!"

There were hidden elements and undercurrents here, which he hadn't time to untangle. It was enough, for now, that men who were at present unknown to him were trying diligently to sink him six-foot underground. They needed a correction of ambition. Their motives could be kicked to light later. Forty thousand dollars?

"I've been waiting days to blow the lid off!" said Banjo Ballinger. "Let's do a job of it!"

"*Your* job?"

"And yours. Marshal Conant dealt you in, giving you that deputy badge. His pistoleers — the Silver Spur crowd — are all deputies. Every damn' one of 'em! Conant's up against the Casa Colorado bunch."

"Who're they?"

"Some tough Mexicans who came here lately. Bandits. No worse, I guess, than Conant's crowd. I'm caught in the middle, both gangs on my neck! So are you, Bishop!"

"You're a hell of a comfort to me!" Bishop said.

Sprinting behind Bishop up the back alley, Banjo Ballinger called, "I keep hearing a jingle on the ground, like dimes an' quarters. Who's throwin' money at us?"

"Nobody," Bishop growled. "Bullet tore my pants pocket. I'm sheddin' loose change every step. Where's the Casa Colorado from here?"

"It's right opposite Mike McCall's beer hall. Here's McCall's." Ballinger cut into a side alley leading back to the street. "There's the Casa, right over — Whooh!" He tucked his head in as a flash and report spat from the jutting front of the unlighted cantina across the street. "I guess they're onto us. Heard your loose change dropping. Hey, don't shoot my ear off!"

"Then flap your ear out o' my way!" said Bishop, and let loose with a gun. He pumped three fast shots, ducked back while broken glass tinkled, and listened with pleasure to a pained curse. "How many of 'em are there?"

"Hard to say. They slipped into town like ghosts in the night, and made the Casa their headquarters. Maybe a dozen, who knows? They come an' go. I can't figure what their *jefe* is up to. He's on the outs with Conant and his crowd. It's a case of thieves falling out!"

Bishop narrowed his eyes meditatively. "Thieves? Conant?" He couldn't quite swallow it. "When thieves fall out, it's usually over sharing the loot. Who took your money — or do you know?"

"I know, all right, though I can't prove it. Conant's pistoleers block me from getting a horse to ride south and investigate." Squatting down on his heels, his back to the alley adobe wall, Banjo Ballinger drew out his tobacco sack and papers. "The boss bandit, over there in the Casa. The *jefe.* That's who stole it. Forty thousand dollars in goldback banknotes!"

He shaped and licked a cigarette, fished forth a match, and looked up into the dark face of the notorious gunfighter.

"If somebody helped me get my money back," he said, "I'd cut it with him. Fifty-fifty. Twenty thousand each if we win. Nothing if we lose. A gamble."

Here was deliberate bait. Bishop gave it due consideration, lasting five seconds. Its chancy aspects appealed to him, as a freelance troubleshooter and as a gambler.

The young Arizona cowman was offering him a deal, daring him to plunge all the way into his affair. This Banjo Ballinger was bucking disaster and death, and badly needed an ace to bolster his forlorn hand. He was desperate, despite the coolness of his eyes; as desperate as a sheepman enticing a lobo's help to save his flock from

39

coyotes.

Everyone who knew anything of Rogue Bishop, of his lobo reputation, knew that he seldom played for less than the total pot, all the stakes, no hedging of bets. No cut with anybody in the winnings unless he chose to be charitable.

"I'll take it on," he said to Ballinger.

After all, poker was out of the question this turmoiled night. And he had a score to settle with the sharpshooter who'd nicked him. And forty thousand dollars . . .

Another shot speared from the Casa Colorado. The bullet whanged off the iron hoop of one of the empty barrels that were stacked beside the beer hall. At the same time, Bishop became aware of activity elsewhere. From where he stood near the mouth of the alley he could view part of the street, and along the far side of it some men stealthily advanced, moving from one shadowed cover to another. The long gleam of a shotgun barrel caught his eye. He had half a mind to fire at it, but wasn't sure about the identities and intentions of the men.

He indicated them to Banjo. "Whose side are they on?"

"Not ours!" Banjo replied. "Nobody's on our side. They're some of Conant's so-called deputies. I bet more of 'em are creeping up the alley back of us, which puts us in the middle."

"Couldn't it be they want in on our crack at the Casa?"

"Sure. They hunger for my forty thousand dollars."

"*Our* forty thousand!"

"They'll try to smoke us out so we draw the fire of the Casa bunch. I know what I'm talking about, Bishop. Conant won't pass up this chance. He wants me killed, but not in a way that'll blot his record as town marshal. The Mexicans yonder get the blame."

"Well, they're not blameless!"

"No. Stole my money. Took a shot at you. They're at war with the Conant crowd." Banjo Ballinger moved barrels out from the wall of the beer hall, setting them as a barricade. The barrels, oak hogsheads, were heavy enough to turn a bullet. "We're in the middle, any way you look at it! Let's dig in for —"

"You handle your own fight, I'll handle mine," Bishop interrupted. He sprang onto an upended barrel, bent his long legs, and leaped upward. He grabbed the top of the wall and hauled himself over it.

Banjo gazed up in wonder at the seemingly effortless agility. "What's the idea?" he called.

"I'm going over the roof," came Bishop's curt response. "You're free to do the same."

"I ain't an antelope! Where'll that roof get you?"

"It'll get me going to the joker in the Casa Colorado who nicked me — where my fight is!"

"Where my money is!"

"That too, now you mention it!"

4

The Casa Colorado was an old building that had undergone enlarging alterations, in accord with Trinidad's growth as a railhead town. An enterprising proprietor had built a two-story addition onto its rear, mainly of slab lumber, cheap and ugly, to serve as a hotel for railroad graders — the pick-and-shovel stiffs, gandy dancers, laborers who couldn't afford to pay for anything better.

It had served its purpose, doubtless giving profit to the proprietor. The graders, forerunners of the rails, had moved on southward with the lengthening roadbed. Now the cramped little rooms had become less exclusive in their type of tenantry, and were falling apart, not constructed for permanence.

A horse corral, enclosed by a high fence also of slab lumber, formed a backyard for the ramshackle hotel. Customers of a rough joint like the Casa Colorado weren't apt to complain of horse smells and flies. Bishop surveyed the place only as a house-breaking problem. To get to it he'd gone over roofs and through backyards, and circled around the plaza, which took time. Now he sought entrance, his mind on the sharpshooter who had nicked him — and on forty thousand dollars. The wound itched. It demanded payment.

Occasionally a few shots cracked from the red-painted front of the unlighted Casa Colorado. Carbines. The men in there, in the cantina, were on the alert, sensing an impending attack. *Hombres del campo.* Free-lance *guerreros* far from home and out of law in two countries, they knew how to fight anywhere.

Other gun reports blared in the street and in the alley across from the Casa Colorado. Banjo Ballinger was evidently still making a stand behind the beer barrels, fired at from three directions — the Casa Colorado, and two contingents of Conant's mob of deputies, one in the street, one coming up the alley.

There were horses in the corral behind the Casa Colorado. Scenting Bishop's presence, they stamped and snorted, snuffy from being penned-up with fodder and water and no exercise. They were good horses, used to hard riding, not accustomed to ease. Their saddles, high-cantled, Mexican, hung on rails. Bishop moved along the outside of the high fence to its abutment against the back of the hotel.

He climbed onto the fence. The horses in the corral froze stockstill, white-eyed, watching him. They were on the edge of milling in noisy panic, noise that would fetch forth their owners. He spoke to them softly in *pocho* Spanish.

"Ho, caballos — ho! . . ." And the earthy words, fondly insulting, familiar to them.

Soothed somewhat, the horses pricked forward their laid-back ears, still watching him suspiciously. Perched on top of the corral fence, he rose to his full height, balancing on the cross-bar, and reached up. His fingers found the rough sill of a second-story window. He hauled himself up to it.

Burglary wasn't his trade, but he was capable of it when circumstances called for house-breaking. Resting his weight on one elbow, he eased the window open and crawled through. The horses in the corral, no more alarmed, fell boredly to nibbling at the hay and at one another.

He crawled into a narrow room that was meagerly furnished with a cot and washstand. A crib for transients able to pay a dollar, and for overnight couples paying more for privacy. The room was unoccupied now, as was all of the hotel, because of the Mexican bandit take-over. The proprietor and guests doubtless had prudently scooted off the premises.

The flimsy floorboards creaked under Bishop's weight. He waited until the next burst of shots drowned out the betraying sound, and trod swiftly to the door of the room. When he gentled the door open, he found that it led onto a skimpily cramped little hallway, a passage running into an inside gallery that was built above the bar of the cantina. The gallery stairs descended to the barroom. Ordinarily, anyone wanting a room simply paid his toll in advance at the bar and went on up, with or without company, seen by everybody in the barroom. There was no privacy in a place like the Casa Colorado.

Bishop crept along the passage to the overhanging gallery. From there, he could see below the dim square of the main front window, bullet-smashed since his shot, and the smaller rectangles of other side windows unbroken as yet.

It was ominously quiet down there in the dark barroom. Then somebody moved. A gun's discharge flared out over the sill of the shattered window. The shooter muttered a Spanish curse, meaning he'd missed. Other voices in the dark laughed briefly, jeering at him. A hard bunch, this. Shrugging, the shooter bent low and scratched a match to a cigarette.

By the light of the match Bishop imprinted a picture of the barroom on his mind. The indefinite outlines of ten or a dozen men showed here and there, crouched below the window sills. They were heavily armed, all of them strung with cartridge bandoleers and double gunbelts, all cuddling carbines readily to shoulders.

One of them shifted over and got a light for himself before the match burned out. The lighted cigarette changed hands, passing along the line. Borrowing fire from it, other dots of burning tobacco glowed in the darkness. A cool bunch, as well as hard — hard as iron — they belonged to the ragged edge of men who challenged death. Freelance *guerreros.* Professional fighters, for pay or plunder.

Their kind weren't strangers to Bishop. He counted his friends and enemies among all classes of men, north and south of the border, without distinction of race, nationality, or degree of lawlessness. A man was as good as his heart and as bad as his intentions, regardless of where or how he happened to get born. The Rio Grande was no barrier to human vices and virtues. It had never barred his own wayward passage, though sometimes it had presented difficulties.

He bit on a fresh cigar, and, drawing his pair of guns, advanced onto the overlooking gallery with a hope that it was more stoutly built than the slab hotel. The hope vanished at his first step.

Poorly braced, the gallery had evidently suffered hard use in its time and nobody had ever seen fit to repair it. It groaned betrayingly, warped floorboards sagging. The glowing cigarettes in the darkness shifted swiftly, all heads twisted around to the sound. A voice rapped a sharp demand.

"Quien es?"

Bishop cocked an ear to that voice. It seemed to have a familiar ring, he wasn't sure. Standing motionless, he listened for more, but the voice was silent. The *guerreros* also were listening, ready to shoot if he didn't promptly respond. They knew where his sound had come from, and probably they were able to discern partly the blur of his figure up on the gallery.

Taking a long risk, he barked, "Freeze, *hombres* — you're covered!"

He didn't expect the bluff to succeed, not with this band of heavily armed desperadoes who dared to penetrate right inside Trinidad and defied the town. In a distant sense their brigandly type carried on the ancient tradition of Spanish men-at-arms, the long-ago adventurers who joined any reckless expedition to loot gold from a vast, unknown land. Three hundred years of Indian infusion, marriage and whatever, certainly had not cooled the hot blood of violence, Bishop knew from personal experience.

All he hoped to gain from his blatant bluff was a thin margin of surprise, a fraction of time to remove himself as a target. That was all he got. A scant two seconds. He sank down flat, while they sprang up, firing.

He poked his guns forward, triggering them downward explosively, fast — heavy, long-barreled guns — causing the *guerreros* to chase across the barroom and scramble over the bar. Their maneuver was smart. He retreated into the upstairs passage of the hotel, in a jump. The shock of his jump left the gallery shaking.

Gunfire roared from below. Splinters flew from the flimsy floor of the gallery, at the spot he had vacated. Bishop reloaded his guns, fingers nimble, experienced. Yet this was a tight jackpot. Very tight. The bar lay directly underneath, where he couldn't sight them — the *guerreros* — let alone shoot back at them.

Smoke from their powder — burned black gunpowder in crude but deadly carbines — rose and acridly fouled the stale air. Their racket infernally assaulted the ear. Bishop caught the sound of squeaking stairs. Some of them, not satisfied with remaining below to riddle the sorry excuse of a gallery, were coming up the steps to kill him at closer quarters — pushing the fight while they had the advantage and blazing their guns like mad at the passage to make him keep his head pulled in.

Out front in the street, the sniping suddenly increased to a volley of gunfire. Men shouted to one another. A rumbling, bumping noise intruded into the uproar. Banjo Ballinger was evidently meeting a load of trouble out there in the alley across the street. This boomtown was getting its lid blown off tonight, for sure, but Bishop doubted if that young Arizona brushpopper was gaining any good from it.

He lined up his cocked guns, watching for the first head to bulge into the bullet-pocked passage. He despised being on the defensive, resented it, as an ace gunmaster with prestige and personal pride to uphold. Outgunned, he had to take it.

In the moment of waiting, he speculated again about the familiar ring of that voice in the barroom below, and about Ballinger's forty thousand dollars, more important. And, lastly, about the rumbling noise outside the Casa Colorado. It sounded like a wooden ball, trundling in the street and coming closer to the Casa. A strange sound.

The gunfire and shouting outside ceased abruptly, as if Marshal Conant's crew of deputies became momentarily hypnotized by an incredible sight. The Mexican warriors stilled, listening, puzzled, on the alert as tigers.

The trundling object hit the front door of the Casa a terrific blow that shook the whole building. It smashed through, and right away there wasn't much door left.

It was a beer barrel, a fifty-five gallon hogshead built heavily of two-inch oak. It rumbled into the barroom like a blundering, monstrous creature, bringing before it the broken remains of the door. Behind it, propelling it onward, a crouching man sang out, "Here I am, Bishop!"

That mad young Arizonian again. Ballinger.

The beer barrel rolled from Bishop's
restricted view. He heard it bang against the
bar. Ballinger raised another yell and loosed
a shot, angering the embattled Mexicans,
who crackled indignant oaths. *Por dios,* a
beer barrel, indeed! An insult.

Bishop snatched the opportunity to vacate
his cover in the passage. Not to retreat back
through the hotel, though. To hell with that
prudent escape, good money being involved
and a bullet-nicked thigh demanding settle-
ment. He jumped forward. Stiffening his
long legs, he landed full-weight on the outer
edge of the gallery.

In his leap he glimpsed murky figures on
the stairs, all of them staring down into the
barroom and raising their carbines. It was
no more than a brief impression, for his
jump had to be fast.

The ramshackle gallery, already over-
loaded by the men crowding its stairs,
strained to the last nail, surrendered under
the pounding force of Bishop's jump on its
edge. It parted company with the wall. It
swayed ponderously, tilting over. The men
on the stairs grabbed hold of the railing,
increasing the strain.

A wooden support broke like a dulled

shot. Parts of the adobe wall, where spiked, crumbled loose, freeing other supporting timbers. The entire contraption then collapsed. It crashed down onto the bar directly beneath.

Above the noise of it, Banjo Ballinger yelled, "Hey, what the goddam — Aw, no! I'm buried!"

"Too bad, buster!"

Bishop didn't linger on his first devastating jump. The gallery sinking under his feet, he rode it down and jumped again. He was spraddled on the barroom floor, catching his balance, when the gallery smashed down onto the bar. He reared up, guns ready for something to shoot at, but it was like hunting strays on a foggy night in the brush. The darkness was aswirl with risen dust. Where the bar had been, there was now a pile of wreckage, under which men squirmed in a tangle, uttering outraged streams of profanity.

A shot lanced from the debris. Bishop shifted out of line of the windows. The shot tempted him to bombard the wreckage in return, but the dusty darkness made any shooting blindly indiscriminate and he didn't want to chance hitting Banjo Ballinger, wherever he was. Banjo had come through usefully when needed, although at this moment nothing more was being heard from him.

"Where in the hell are you, Ballinger?" Bishop called.

"In hell is right!" came Banjo's panting retort, along with wrenching bumps. "I did okay till you booted the shebang down on me! I'm up to my neck in busted timbers!"

"Claw clear soon's you can!"

"What d'ya think I'm doing?" The bumping continued.

"Need any help?"

"Guess I can make it. These knife-blade *orejanos,* though, they're clawing after me! Watch out! Their *jefe* — Risa —"

"Who?" Bishop cut in, recollecting the voice that he had heard in the barroom. The vaguely familiar ring; he placed it now, hearing the name. His sharp senses keened instantly. "De Risa, you mean? Don Ricardo de Risa? He's their *jefe?"*

"I figured you knew that."

"The hell you did!"

He had got flimflammed. He — Rogate Bishop, master of misleading arts, professional shark — bamboozled by an amateur. Hoodwinked. Manipulated like a dupe. Lured unknowingly into an outright fight with an old enemy, the most formidable,

54

most dangerous man he had ever crossed in all his violence-smeared career: Don Ricardo de Risa. The Laughing One, as he was known fondly in Mexico, less fondly north of the border where the wanted posters proclaimed rewards for his capture, dead or alive.

"You know him?" Banjo Ballinger inquired, too innocently, squirming to free himself. "Personally?"

"We're acquainted," said Bishop. Which was considerably within the realm of understatement. For years, he and Don Ricardo de Risa had intermittently clashed in a personal feud, as was known. He peered dourly into the murk, seeing nothing, only hearing the noises made by men scrabbling out from underneath the collapsed gallery.

"Rico, you cuss, are you alive?"

"Alive and looking for you!" crackled the response, and again a gun whammed in Bishop's direction, bare inches too high, causing him to crouch lower to the floor.

Don Ricardo de Risa, one-time swank officer, Mexican revolutionary general, all-time rascal turned bandit, was very plainly in a murderous frame of mind. Two countries had declared him outlawed, which hardly bothered him. Bounty hunters left him alone, shrugging off the rewards on his head. He was too fast on the gun, too wily to fall into traps.

There were sufficient reasons for Don Ricardo to seek Bishop over gunsights — as many reasons as Bishop had for entertaining similar designs against him. Still, it struck Bishop that the don's present animosity seemed particularly malignant. Something extraordinary lay behind it. That bullet in the street had been meant to kill him, no warning, a raw action that didn't fit the don's subtle nature and sense of finesse.

In the past, their every meeting had sparked a battle of wits. They had pulled outrageous tricks on each other, their feud a deadly game, but they played it under tacitly recognized rules, in a spirit of wicked humor and grim mischief. For one of them to attempt a graceless assassination of the other, without at least a preliminary gesture or word of challenge, was beyond all decency. It implied that Don Ricardo de Risa, self-styled *aristo* of refined breeding, had perhaps finally coarsened into becoming a crude killer.

"Son of a goat!" Bishop hammered shots at where the don's muzzle-flash had showed.

"Animalucho!" The don had already shifted. His gun spurted from a different spot. "Coyote!"

5

A hail came from outside the Casa Colorado. "Bishop!" Marshal Conant's voice. "Bishop, what's doin' in there?"

"Come in and see for yourself!" Bishop answered. "Bring a lantern!" he added sardonically, and went to warily stalking his elusive foe around the barroom. A lighted lantern in here wouldn't last two ticks.

The don's warriors, extricating themselves from beneath the collapsed gallery, lay low in the dark, confusedly trying to sort out which was which of the unseen duelists.

Banjo Ballinger, noisily heaving scrap lumber, panted, "Lost my gun! Bishop, don't let Conant's bunch come in! Not till I find my gun, anyhow. An' don't you kill Risa! He's the hombre who knows where our forty thousand dollars went to! He —"

"I know also where a certain badge went!" cut in Don Ricardo from wherever he was. "*Mira!* 'Our' forty thousand?" A biting laugh. "The money went to a slimy scoundrel. The badge went to a coyote — Rogue Bishop — who has sunk so low that he sells his services to a renegade lawman!"

Bishop's wrath soared. "You goddam liar!" He fired again, intolerably insulted. To be shot without warning was bad enough, but to be slandered on top of it — that was going altogether too far. "I'll kill you, Rico!"

"Not after I kill you, traitor!"

"Bishop!" broke in Banjo urgently. "Risa! Call it off, will you? Listen what's going on out there! They've got us nailed in a fix, dammit!"

There were hushed mutterings and muffled noises of a mob of men massing closely around the building on all sides. Tom Conant's deputies, seizing the opportunity, had closed in, and apparently they had gathered plenty of volunteers to back them, the town aroused up in arms against the impudent band of brigands.

A voice rose above the sounds. Surprisingly, it was the piping voice of the little veterinary, Doc Sunday. Yet it immediately gained listening attention from the encircling mob, as if it spoke with Jehovah-like thunder.

"Citizens of Trinidad! I call on every man here to give full support to Marshal Conant! The law must be upheld. That Mexican cantina is a foul den of crime. Destroy it! Burn it down! Shoot the criminals as they slink out! Show no mercy to such rats!"

With the ending of the inflaming and somewhat pious speech, a thoughtful silence settled inside the embattled Casa Colorado, which Banjo Ballinger was the first to break.

"It's a set-up, Bishop," he said. "Conant set it, giving you that deputy badge, letting Risa see you take it. He's on the shoot for Risa. He used you, Bishop."

"You mean *you* did!"

"Conant did it better. Played one ace against another. You against Risa. Then he moves in with his deputies, like now, for the jackpot. Forty thousand dollars."

"That jackpot appears to have more bright specimens gunning for it than wasps around a syrup jug," commented Bishop.

It didn't sit at all well with him that he had been juggled into playing the part of a cat's-paw. Twice juggled, in fact, since his arrival at Trinidad. First by Banjo Ballinger, then by Marshal Conant. It made him seriously wonder if his wits had dulled.

He raised his voice. "Rico! You hear what Ballinger said? Quit shooting at me, and I'll do you the same favor — for the time being. We've got to smoke it out of here, damned *pronto,* or we're cooked! Meet me at the front door. You, too, Ballinger. Stay with me!"

Stay with me, he meant, because you, Ballinger, know the layout behind all this murderous intrigue. Because I'm now committed, up to my neck, and aim to ride close-herd on you till the what's-what and who's-who comes clear. A strictly practical purpose of self-interest. Bishop very rarely engaged himself in any to-do except for its prospects of personal profit. As a professional troubleshooter, his second trade to gambling, he took a detached view toward people's troubles.

They met at the smashed front door, the three of them, in prickly truce. In the faint light coming in from the street, Don Ricardo de Risa looked somewhat damaged and worn. Usually trim and debonair, flamboyantly dandyish, the crush of the gallery had marred his elegance.

Even his swarthily handsome face hadn't escaped unscathed, one side of it grazed and dirty. His thin line of black mustache lacked the fine points of meticulously waxed ends. They spiked frayed, smudged, rather clownish. Bishop snorted a short laugh at him.

"You look banged-up, Rico! Something fall on you?"

■ ■ ■ ■

The don's dark eyes held a quiet glitter, in which bloody enmity and evil humor mingled. His slimly erect body fell into a naturally graceful pose, one hand resting negligently on his hip, the other on the butt of a holstered gun. Don Ricardo could always be counted on to cut a dash, under whatever circumstances, while at the same time be perfectly ready to deal out sudden death if the occasion and chance warranted it.

"I notice you do not wear your badge openly," he murmured with silken politeness. "Could it be that you are ashamed of it?"

"You mention that goddam badge just one more time, and I'll bend a gunbarrel over your bonnet!" Bishop promised acidly. "I seem to have got myself rigged into a cussed mess of yours. The only part I like about it is the money."

"You haven't changed in that respect, Rogue!"

"Nor you! Ballinger claims you stole forty thousand dollars from him. Frankly, I aim to get it back."

"For a split in it?"

"Why else?"

The don's teeth flashed whitely in a broad and comradely smile. "You restore my faith in the predacity of human nature! Particularly your predatory nature!" His English was fluent, marked by only a trace of Spanish accent.

Perhaps it was true that he had attended famous schools in his youth, European, expensive. Perhaps not. He possessed the facile talents of a smooth charlatan, and a flair for genteel elegance. Beneath the slightly gaudy trappings of a blood-proud hidalgo, a caballero, he remained simply an outright scoundrel, as Bishop knew only too well.

"Forty thousand dollars, American, is a lot of money. A beautiful bundle of goldbacks! I had it in my hands for a while, but —"

"Never mind that now," Bishop interrupted. "Tell your warriors to slip out back and saddle-up their nags. We've got to bust out, Rico! They're readying to roast us! Hear 'em? They're sloshing coal oil on the walls."

"They'll have the back alley covered," Banjo Ballinger pointed out. "We can't make it there. They'll slaughter us!"

Don Ricardo beamed his smile at Bishop.

"*Amigo,* this person underestimates us! You and I have blasted out of some tight spots — together, though not in amiable accord. In our private fraternity, if I may use the term —"

"Ah, shut it off! It's no time for flowery talk."

"Sorry. Your plan is the same as mine, eh? I and my men will get our horses ready in the rear corral. Meantime, you create a diversion, drawing the enemy into the street. Which will clear the back alley for our break. Right?"

"Pretty close," Bishop acknowledged.

"I and my men will wait for you, of course," added the don brightly.

"Of course you will."

Don Ricardo departed rearward, taking with him his warriors, whispering to them as they slipped out the back door.

"Hell's windmills!" Banjo Ballinger exclaimed, staring incredulously at Bishop after they were gone. "He'll skip off and leave us in the lurch! D'you trust that stinker?"

Bishop shifted his chewed, unlighted cigar. "Yeah," he murmured, peering out at the armed mob in the street. "I trust Rico — as far as I'd trust an Apache horse thief on a moonless night, just about, or less!"

63

"Then why — ?"

"I've got my reasons."

Shots blared behind the Casa Colorado. A horse squealed. From the street in front came another yelled query, in a different voice.

"Bishop? We'll finish the job in there! Come on out, if you're able."

"And get your head blown off!" muttered Banjo. "That's Shang Tate, the feller with the chisel chin an' big teeth. The one you booted. Top trigger in Conant's bunch."

Bishop nodded. From the sounds out back, he judged that Don Ricardo and his crew were set to make their break out of the hotel corral, leaving him and Ballinger in the lurch to cover their getaway. He didn't have any illusions that they intended to wait. It was too much to expect. The don couldn't resist that enticing temptation to pay off some old scores, with trickery that commonly rated as treachery — but which, between him and Bishop, was typical of their strictly private feud.

And Bishop didn't have any compunctions in twisting the trick to double-cross the don. "I'm able to come on out!" he hailed in answer to Shang Tate. "So's Ballinger. But what for? If you and the mob mean business, get to the back corral where the break-out's due, while we block 'em here!"

Armed citizens swarmed through the side alley of the Casa Colorado, racing to the rear. A straggle of Conant's deputies followed them, despite Shang Tate's and Marshal Conant's shouts of forbiddance. Shang Tate's prestige had suffered a humbling blow, and Conant's authority was evidently not total. They wanted the street in front strongly guarded, but they weren't able to control the whole force of trigger-eager deputies.

So much to the good. Bishop, with Ballinger on his heels, strode to the back door to witness the effect of his warning to the mob. He could already hear it. When he peered out, the corral was a dust-swirling madhouse.

The surrounding attackers fired through the chinks in the high slab fence, blazing without aim into the corral where saddled horses plunged and reared in squealing panic. Some of the *guerreros,* on foot and clinging to bridle reins, dodging hoofs, tried riskily to return the fire without hitting one another. Those who were mounted had all they could handle, staying with their saddles. Two or three of the horses, riderless and on the loose, bucked around the corral with heads tucked low and tails high, adding to the wild pandemonium.

Bishop glimpsed a blurred silhouette, a slender rider magnificently mastering his tossing seat while managing at the same time to keep a gun spurting. No mistaking that superb horseman, that acrobatic *pistolero.*

"This way, Rico!" he barked. "The cantina — through the cantina, quick!"

"Coming!" Don Ricardo's plunging horse loomed closer, fighting the spade-bit, the don forcing it tight-reined and spurred to his will.

"Don't forget to duck at the door!" Bishop sprang aside and into the milling ruckus of the corral. "Grab a horse for yourself, Ballinger — we're going out with this bunch!"

"They're bandits! Risa robbed —"

"If you can pick better company, go to it!"

Hoofs thundered on the cantina floor, gouging and scarring it. Tables and chairs crashed, overturned, broken underfoot. In its past the Casa Colorado had undoubtedly suffered the visits of boisterous riders who brought in their horses, but probably never this many at one time.

By some miracle Don Ricardo entered the

back door without dismounting or cracking his head. His followers had to drag and bully their animals through. Bishop, making connection with the snapping reins of a riderless horse, ran it to the door, on the way colliding into Banjo Ballinger and a captive sorrel that had lost its last grain of sense.

Stamping horses and cursing men choked the battered cantina. The front exit was blocked by the don, whose mount, showing the whites of its eyes, refused to budge, disliking the looks of the smashed-in door.

Bishop checked his borrowed horse and swung up into the high-cantled Mexican saddle. The stirrup leathers were notched somewhat short for his long legs, but they had to do for now. He jostled up behind the don to help him onward and clear the exit. No good. He reached over and hit the don's temperamental animal a mighty swipe guaranteed to shift a Missouri mule, and Don Ricardo barely got his head down in time to miss the doorframe, going out, Bishop close on the tail, Ballinger next. Then every horse in the cantina took the notion to follow.

They streamed forth, dodging the empty hitchrack out front, the *guerreros* mounting on the run as they hit the street. Flashing by the side alley, Bishop slung a shot into it and another at a dim figure crouched in a dark doorway with a rifle. Shang Tate, he hoped, seeing the rifle waver and sag.

Not all of Conant's deputies had run around to the back to take part in the corral blockade. Those who did were now returning, with some of the citizens. They had caught on to the enemy maneuver a moment late. None appeared sold on jumping into the way of the string of shooting horsemen. Marshal Conant, if still around, wasn't setting any hazardous example. Nor Shang Tate. And certainly not Doc Sunday.

Bishop ran his horse abreast of Don Ricardo, riding out through the fringe of town where doors hurriedly slammed shut as the cavalcade clattered by. The gunfire had aroused all Trinidad. "We worked that trick okay," he commented.

It brought him a level stare from dark eyes in which rancor mingled with wry respect. "*Your* trick! It would have worked better for me if I had guessed what you had in mind! I lost two of my men in that corral. You and Ballinger are riding their horses. And I got a bullet through my sombrero!"

The high-peaked sombrero was a dashingly elegant and expensive article of headgear, richly encrusted with gold and silver braid. The don's taste in attire was fastidious: short jacket over silk shirt, frogged pants, sash, silver spurs. He dressed the part of a *charro* dandy, *meterse á caballero*, though at present showing signs of considerable wear and tear. The silk shirt was soiled, the jacket had a rip down the back, and the sash looked as if he had used it to hobble a horse. His thin line of black mustache needed trimming. He wasn't his usual debonair self, in appearance nor in disposition.

"Two men lost," he repeated, examining his punctured sombrero, his chief concern.

"Let's not waste any regrets," said Bishop, taking a practical view. "Just so you didn't lose forty thousand dollars!"

Replacing the sombrero on his sleek head, Don Ricardo uttered a brief and mirthless laugh. "Rogue, you're too late. This time your nose for gains had led you astray down a cold trail. That money is long gone," he said bitterly. "I lost it nearly a week ago!"

"The hell you say! All the forty thousand?"

"Every dollar of it!"

Bishop believed him. Only the loss of plunder could account for the don's soured disposition. "Damn!" he muttered, the fading prospects of profit darkening his own mood. "Must be you're slipping, Rico. Getting dull."

"Don't strain my temper, Rogue!" The dark eyes flashed dangerously. "I am as sharp as ever! And as fast!"

"As touchy, anyhow, or more. I'm not forgetting how you nicked me in the leg tonight, from cover."

"I've told you why."

"Doesn't make it any less sore. Well, let's cool off and keep moving. We don't want Conant's mob on our tails."

6

Northward along the Purgatoire they drew in below the skyline of the long ridge that overlooked the river and the new steel tracks of the Atchison, Topeka & Santa Fe Railroad. They loosened cinches, aired their saddles, and lighted up cigarettes, keeping ears cocked for sounds of possible pursuit from Trinidad.

Bishop held close watch on them, acquainted with their hard breed, the kind of desperadoes who followed the fortunes of Don Ricardo de Risa or any other capable leader. Their kind paid scant reverence to human life, and they had no love for gringos. There was the smoldering recollection that this vast land had once been a province of New Spain and of Mexico.

The Purgatoire, so named by French voyageurs, and called the Picketwire in careless American vernacular, was actually the Rio de las Animas Perdidas — River of Lost

Souls. Westward rose the immense Sangre de Cristos — Blood of Christ Mountains, red at sunset — towering above such far-flung places as Santo Domingo, San Ildefonso, Tierra Amarilla. And Santa Fe, ancient capital of New Mexico. Santa Fe, La Villa Real de la Santa Fe de San Francisco, the Royal City of the Holy Faith of Saint Francis. Spanish names to jog the memory.

The railroad tracks followed the trail carved by the American traders, intrepid hucksters who had yearly persisted in venturing forth from Independence with cumbersome great wagons full of goods for sale to the Santa Fe market. A journey of nigh a thousand miles, hostile Indians merely one of the problems, bad weather the worst. The deep ruts of the wagon wheels could still be seen, resembling from a distance the strands of a frayed rope, for many a wagon had pulled out of line to beat the others to market. The Old Santa Fe Trail had bred competition, traders being what they were.

The whole country was soaked in a history of struggle and violence, from early savagery to Spanish conquest, to the American invasion and its conflicts. The dark, silent land seemed to be brooding, like a behemoth raised on bloodshed and waiting for havoc again. Civilization couldn't ever tame it. It was too old in its ways.

Lighting a cigar, Bishop rid himself of a feeling of depression, meantime seeing to it that nobody got behind him. His depression he laid to the loss of the money, knowing it wasn't strictly true. Many times the feeling had assailed him in lonely camps at night, stars diamond-clear, earth black. The pensive *coraje* — that impossible wish to cut loose and soar above life.

"Now," he began, "about your forty thousand dollars, Rico. Just what —"

"*My* forty thousand!" broke in Banjo Ballinger. "I'll tell you the what of it, Bishop!"

"Go ahead. So far, all I've heard about it is scraps and pieces. Let him talk, Rico, will you? *Por favor.*"

Don Ricardo shrugged a shoulder. "No objection."

"I drove a beef herd up here from Arizona," Banjo said. "Some of it belonged to neighbors and friends o' mine back home. They trusted me. Trusted I'd sell their cows for 'em along with mine, at a right price. They —"

"Cut the music and get to the point!"

"All right. I sold the herd to Doc Sunday, top price, cash on the line."

Bishop raised his dark eyebrows. "Doc

73

Sunday?"

Banjo nodded. "Doc's a lot more'n just a vet. He owns town and ranch property, and he's a stock dealer, pretty big. He's contracted to deliver beef to the railroad construction camps, besides to the Mescalero Indian Reservation. He needed my herd to fill his contracts. So he paid me tops, no haggling."

"And the cash went missing?"

"Yeah. In a stage holdup next day. This Risa bandit, he took it — forty thousand dollars in goldback federal banknotes!"

Don Ricardo eyed Banjo meditatingly. "I should shoot you, but sometimes a fool has his uses," he murmured. "And you do have reason for grievance, after all." To Bishop, he said, "So have I!"

"Get it off your chest."

"In plain facts, a prominent citizen of Trinidad informed me that the stage to Santa Fe would carry a large sum of cash in the express box," the don related. "I was told that the owner of the cash would ride the stage with it. He was described as an Arizona hombre who had a scar on his face. My informant — the prominent citizen — bargained for a share of the cash, of course. He also wanted the owner of it killed, as a precaution against later flarebacks. The

74

thing looked simple, and easy —"

"But you had different ideas," Bishop interposed. "Ideas that didn't match with your prominent citizen's bargain. Stick to the plain facts, Rico!"

Don Ricardo de Risa inclined his head in shameless acknowledgment. "I had no intention of sharing the plunder with him, no! Oh, you mean the man with the scar, on the stage? He got killed in the holdup, reaching for a shotgun." The don bent a glance to Banjo. "Who *was* that idiot?"

"Not me," said Banjo. "I'd planned to take that stage, but then I met Vada Conant, and — Never mind that. I shipped my money on ahead, and stayed over. The man you killed in the holdup was the mayor of Trinidad. He was going down to Santa Fe on business. He had a scar a bit like mine."

"So!" exclaimed Don Ricardo. "That was why the town was so hostile, keeping me holed-up in that miserable cantina! I didn't dare show a light! They knew who pulled the holdup and shot the mayor. At least, Marshal Conant knew. But he couldn't gather enough guns to come at me. So he enlisted Bishop —"

"Watch that, Rico!"

"He tricked you," the don amended. "Tricked you into taking a badge, in the light, for me to see. What was I to think, other than that you were siding with the law against me?"

"Okay, I accept your apology for that bullet."

"You deserve a thousand bullets! I should have aimed higher!"

Bishop grinned sparely. They were on the familiar grounds of mutual insults and unpaid grudges. "What happened after you robbed the stage and shot the wrong man? You took the express box, didn't you?"

"Certainly! But then my men and I ran into trouble, riding south. Posses sprang up everywhere, as if warned. Raton Pass was blocked. We broke up and scattered. The prominent Trinidad citizen had arranged to meet us in a buckboard. As a last resort I met him at the rendezvous and gave him the express box — it was unwieldy and conspicuous on my saddle. He could get it past the posses, covered under a blanket in his buckboard. No questions. A man of prestige, you understand."

"He rooked you?"

Don Ricardo winced at the memory. "Yes! I planned to catch up and take it from him later on the Trinidad road. But the thieving scoundrel turned off the road somewhere and eluded me! He got safely home to Trinidad with the express box. And there, curse him, he was able to defy me! Refused to give me my share of the money!"

His wrath brought again the grin to Bishop's hard mouth. It was rare that Don Ricardo de Risa, master of devious trickery, could be double-crossed successfully. Very rare indeed. When it did happen he was indignant. It injured his self-esteem, the puffed ego that he had to sustain as a leader of violent men, warriors whose critical standard was mercenary, a simple matter of loot. Let the leader fail, the warriors quit him.

This particular double-cross smelled of careful planning. Somebody had alerted the law beforehand, else the posses wouldn't have been so fast on tap after the stage holdup. Raton Pass, the route south to New Mexico from Colorado . . . blocked? That had taken forethought.

"I have waited and watched to get at that swindling scoundrel!" declared the don. His dark eyes gleamed wickedly. "He surrounds himself with gunmen, but some day I'll get him!"

"Marshal Conant, you mean?" Banjo Ballinger inquired.

"No, you stone-headed gringo! I mean Doc Sunday!"

Banjo stared. "Doc? My friend, the only friend I've got in Trinidad? I don't believe it!"

"That," said the don icily, "is your privilege. Doc Sunday was my informant — the man in the buckboard, who took the express box containing your forty thousand dollars! He's still got it! He planned the holdup!" The dark eyes glittered. There was no mistaking the don's sincerity. "Doc Sunday isn't your friend, any more than I am! He's a crook! I've had dealings with him before, selling him cattle which, frankly, were stolen — and he knew it! He could afford paying you top price for your herd, knowing he'd steal back the money! He's done it before. This time he got greedy and hogged it all."

Banjo clapped a hand to his forehead. "Damn my thick skull! All the time I've thought it was Conant — him and his deputies. I'm sure glad, for Vada's sake —"

"Restrain your gladness! Marshal Conant isn't any angel. He's a crook, too!"

"Cripes! Is everybody in Trinidad crooked?"

"I wouldn't know. I do know that Doc Sunday is secretly the boss, and Conant is his tool. Conant's deputies take their orders from Doc. The only reason why Doc didn't order the deputies to pull the stage robbery is, he'd have had to pay them a share. So he used me — *me!* Then he tried to wipe me out, he and Conant and the deputies!"

Bishop shook his head, partly in admiration. "Smart little bastard! I was used, too, taking that badge. We both got rooked, Rico! So did Ballinger! Doc's sitting nice on forty thousand dollars, clear profit. Wonder where he keeps it?"

"Are you suggesting that we join forces against him?" inquired Don Ricardo. "A formidable task, we being far out of law! That whole town is hostile to us! Still," he admitted, "it's an intriguing challenge, if that's what you have in mind."

Before Bishop could reply, Banjo Ballinger said, "My cows are in the railroad holding pens, waiting for a cattle train to ship them north. Doc Sunday holds a clear bill of sale on them. Knowing what I know now, I'd love chucking him into a pen! Those critters are wild, combed out of cactus country. When I paid off my trail crew in Trinidad, they all swore they'd never again drive an Arizona herd. Trouble all the way! Do you two hotshots have any idea how to get my money? I'm dead broke!"

■ ■ ■ ■

Bishop and Don Ricardo exchanged looks, both seeking to read the other's mind. The don smiled. Imps of deviltry danced in his eyes. He could never pass up a dare, spoken or implied, no matter how harebrained it might be — especially from Bishop.

"Well, *amigo?* Shall we try for it together?"

The proposal amounted to a mockery as well as a dare. Neither of them having any illusions about the other, both took for granted the faithless nature of such a pact. It could be nothing else than a false truce between them, a joining of forces purely for the sake of cash stakes, trickery lurking in wait for the opportune time. A competitive glint crept into Bishop's deepset gray eyes.

He nodded toward Banjo Ballinger. "What about him? He's got an interest in it."

"We'll cut him in if we get the money — if he earns a share," replied the don. "That money belongs now to whoever can take it. We'll need any help we can get."

"You're mighty generous," said Banjo with sarcasm. His face, as he studied the notorious pair, expressed in part his inner thoughts about them. They would work together against the common enemy, sure, as long as high stakes were in sight. A robbed and busted cowman couldn't ask for more formidable allies on his side.

They would fight like devils for their mutual cause. The payoff would come when and if they finally got within reach of the stakes. A third party wouldn't stand anywhere then, in the inevitable showdown between those two.

Still, there was always a faint chance. It wasn't unknown for a nervy terrier to dart in and snatch off the bone, while a couple of wolfish hounds circled each other in a fight over it.

"I'll go along," Banjo said to them.

They didn't look at him, gave no sign of hearing him, engrossed in their private challenge. He hardly counted in their reckonings. He merely happened to be the owner of the money, or had been till he lost it. And the money itself took second place now to the challenge. The game was more important than the stakes.

"Shall we, Rogue?" Don Ricardo asked, smiling.

Bishop debated a moment longer. He didn't believe that his wits had grown dull. Yet he had got hoodwinked in Trinidad, which shook slightly his belief in himself. The don had fared worse, got neatly cheated. He suspected that the don felt the same uneasy edge of uncertainty. It required a test, a perilous and difficult test, to restore complete self-confidence. And that was even more important than the game. Bishop nodded.

"We'll give it a whirl, Rico."

"Bueno!"

The twist to Don Ricardo's smile confirmed Bishop's surmise. The don wanted the toughest test possible, double hazard, Bishop pitted against him, Trinidad pitted against them both. He had to prove to himself that he was as sharp as ever.

So did Bishop, on the thin end of the odds: Don Ricardo and his warriors, Trinidad and its swarm of corrupt lawmen. He was alone except for Ballinger. He assured himself that he generally performed best in the worst pinch. The assurance was necessary.

"First, Rico, tell off your *ladrones* they're not to gun me in the back! Nor Ballinger."

A rapped order, and the don said, "It is done."

"Next, we figure out a move to catch Doc Sunday. We've got to know where he's stashed the loot. It could be anywhere, maybe buried outside Trinidad, some place only he knows."

The don shook his head. "No, I'm positive he took the express box into Trinidad. I tracked him later, after shaking off those infernal posses. He drove the rig straight back to town without a halt, at a fast run, knowing I'd soon come after him for the money."

"So it's there in Trinidad," Bishop said, "and our job's to find it. The quickest way is to catch Doc Sunday and make him tell where."

"No, he's too slippery, Rogue — far too crafty an old fox to catch! Doc Sunday is the undercover master, the real boss of Trinidad. He owns Marshal Conant, body and soul. The gunmen deputies guard Doc day and night, I discovered to my cost! They're all in his pay, like Conant."

Banjo Ballinger, regarding Tom Conant as his future father-in-law, shifted uncomfortably. He was on the outs with Conant, but disliked hearing him described as a renegade lawman by a Mexican bandit. He knew Conant was crooked, yet a tangled loyalty caused him to demand, "Prove it, Risa!"

Ignoring him, Don Ricardo de Risa said to Bishop, "We would need fifty men to go in and capture Doc Sunday. And fifty more to go in again for the money, all of Trinidad shooting at us. Impossible!" He spread his hands eloquently. "The town is an armed camp. We were lucky to get out alive. We surprised them. I was holed in. They would not be surprised again. They'll be on the *cuidado* now, especially Conant's deputies."

"Don't tell me you're quitting, Rico! Then I'd know you've lost your nerve, too, along with your brains!"

"Oh, no, no, Rogue! Never let that be said of me, though I live to a doddering old age, which I doubt! I have a plan, an idea, rather. You may not like it, but I see it as the only solution to our problem."

"I bet it's a beaut!"

"H'm?" The word "beaut" had not yet attached itself to the don's vocabulary. "Beautiful, perhaps not. Effective, perhaps yes. Oblique. Devious. To get that money, we must use oblique methods, a devious attack —"

"Cut the cackle and get to corn! You've got a dirty notion in mind. Spill it!"

7

Don Ricardo sighed. He enjoyed his own eloquence and was apt to get carried away on flowery flights of verbosity. It was one of his few weaknesses, an offshoot of vanity.

"We can strike at Doc Sunday through Conant," he said, regretfully discarding further preamble. "Get a hold on Conant and make him talk."

"Talk about what?" Bishop inquired. "It's a safe bet Doc Sunday hasn't told him or anybody else where he's hidden that express box."

"It stands to reason he wouldn't," conceded the don. "My thought is, Conant has knowledge of Doc Sunday's secrets. He must, being Doc's bought lawman. The concealed crimes — robbery, murder, dealings in stolen cattle . . ." He laughed. "A master criminal, that little vet! We of the wild bunch know him! We don't trust him, but we —"

"Stick to the point! Where does Conant come in?"

"To stop Conant from exposing him, Doc Sunday could be screwed into giving us the money!"

"Blackmail!" Bishop spat. "I've never sunk to that!"

"Call it anything you want. It's an idea. Fight fire with fire. Doc Sunday makes use of any weapon whatever. Can we afford to be squeamish, as heavily outnumbered as we are, a small band of outlaws against Trinidad? *Bien está!* If you have a better idea, I'm ready to listen."

At times, usually in the dead of night, alone at a sheltered campfire or sleepless in some cowtown hotel room, it occurred to Bishop that the flow of his moral life might be drifting downstream. He committed acts which he would have shunned doing in years past. He had grown more and more to tolerate all the vices of mankind, including his own. Morality was a blurred word. What he had left, had retained and hoped he would always retain, was the bare skeleton of a personal code.

"How would we get a hold on Conant?" he inquired.

The don flashed his white-toothed smile. "Through his daughter! I've seen her.

86

Charming young girl. A father is a fool, willing to sacrifice himself for the safety of his only child, and I'm sure Conant is no exception. We abduct her! That's where Ballinger earns his share. He's on close terms with her, I've noticed. All he has to do —"

He broke off, to rap swiftly at Banjo Ballinger, "Don't draw your gun on me! I'll kill you!"

With a sweep of his long arm Bishop shoved the furious Arizona brushpopper back on his heels. "He can do it! Keep your head!" To Don Ricardo, he growled, "That part of your idea is too lowdown for us!"

The don frowned, drawing himself up, hidalgo haughty. "She would not be harmed! We would simply use her as a hold on Conant. A hostage. Surely you don't think I would —"

"That's just what I do think, you tomcat Lothario!"

"You go too far, Rogue! I resent it!" The don's stiff resentment rang a bit hollow. He could never be trusted where a pretty girl was concerned. Another of his little weaknesses, though he held the Latin view of it as a strength, virile and proudly masculine. He paused, alert. "What noise is that?"

The noise was a growing rumble, metallic, such as no hoofed animals ever made. It was interspersed with heavy chugging. A beam of light cut into the night sky.

"Train coming over the grade," Banjo said somberly. "A cattle train, to take on my herd in the loading pens. It's overdue, running behind time."

"It doesn't sound hurried."

"No, because the engineer's got to take it slow on the bends, hauling a string of empty cars. They'd jump the tracks. When he hits the downgrade here he'll cut the throttle and crawl real slow into Trinidad."

"Why?"

"To keep from scaring the daylights out of those cattle in the loading pens, naturally! The critters would bust the pens down if he went roaring in, any fool knows that. At night, the headlight glaring and steam hissing — man! No pens built could hold 'em. The engineer knows he must ease in, wait for daylight, then gentle his train up alongside the pens. Even so, Doc Sunday's punchers won't have any soft job loading my steers. They're plenty ornery to start with."

Chewing on his cigar, Bishop contemplated the oncoming beam of light. It traversed wide arcs as the locomotive climbed around the curves of the roadbed.

"Ever stick up a train, Rico?" he asked.

"Not an empty cattle train, if that is what you mean," disclaimed the don.

"That's my meaning. We're going to take this one."

Banjo stared. "What reason?"

"You just gave the reason. Make your steers break loose and stampede through town, and there'd be some considerable excitement, I bet."

"Sure would!"

Bishop shifted his cigar. "In the excitement we could probably get into Doc Sunday's office and search for the money. Or catch Doc there and hustle him out of town while everybody's busy dodging cows. It's worth trying. We won't get a better chance."

"How would we get out?" Banjo asked. "We'll be afoot, dodging cows like the town folk."

"There are some horses in Doc's livery, mine one of 'em. A few of us might have to ride double, but not far. Rico can leave three or four of his men here to pick up these horses after we board the train, and meet us outside town. How about it, Rico?"

"I still think my plan is best," Don Ricardo demurred. "Yours is full of risks. It would be much easier to —"

"Quit digging for excuses to ring that girl in on the party!" Bishop flung at him. He tightened cinch, stepped into the saddle, and gave the wide brim of his hat a tug, watching the headlight become a glaring orb rounding the final curve. "Ballinger, are you game to ride that rattler into Trinidad with me?"

"You've talked me into it, Bishop! Just us two?"

"Yeah. The bold de Risa has run out of sand!"

The locomotive hissed steam, slowing for the long downgrade ahead. Clashing brake couplings and the grind of wheels drowned the hoofbeats of horsemen circling in to canter alongside the empty cars as near as they could force their unwilling mounts. Being what they were, the riders chose to risk spills rather than attempt jumping the train on foot; high-heeled boots and spurs weren't fit for that task.

Don Ricardo, furiously insulted, was coming along with his men, less those detailed to pick up the horses. What he might do about the insult later was a matter of speculation. Bishop had figured that the don would come along — he couldn't bear to be left out, that wicked daredevil.

The engineer poked his head out of the cab to scan the forward right-of-way. The fireman rested on his coal scoop, speed cut down for the cattle train's quiet entry into town — or as quiet as possible, so as not to stir up the dozing cattle in the railroad loading pens. This was where an engine driver earned some slight right to the title of engineer, though he might understand little of his locomotive's workings.

A brakeman clambered up from the tail-end caboose car and came stepping along the jiggling catwalk over the empty cattle cars, lighted lantern in hand. Three cars up, he stopped short, bewildered by the sight of horsemen jumping onto the train. The jerking of his head meant that he was shouting at them, but the wind tore his voice away.

He broke into a trot, gesturing, swinging his lantern; a trot on the catwalk that only a brakeman or an experienced hobo was capable of doing — a dozen long steps and a skip to the next car. A tiny gun-flash blinked from one of the reckless riders cantering in the darkness.

The brakeman found that he was swinging a dead lantern, bullet-smashed by a humorous crackshot. He dived down and spread himself flat on the catwalk. Prudently, he stayed huddled there. Cowpunchers on a hooraw were rough playmates. He wanted no part in whatever crack-brain prank these night-riding saddle-sinners were up to. Two others of the train crew, emerging from the caboose, elected to follow suit when bullets whined above their heads.

The engineer gaped as a wild-eyed and terrified horse almost spilled itself against the steel pistons and wheels of the chugging locomotive. The rider of the horse leaned far over, kicking loose his stirrups. He became a black apparition, leaping aboard the cab, his horse bolting off free.

The fireman straightened up, eyes popping, raising his coal scoop in confused defense. Train robberies were not uncommon, but this was unique: sticking up a string of empty cattle cars. Senseless.

"S-say, you!" stuttered the engineer to the tall intruder. He groped behind him for a socket wrench. "Wh-what's the idea?" Finding the wrench, a ten-pound shillelagh, he drew courage from it, wielding it overhead. "Git out o' my cab!"

"Don't be unfriendly, brother. We're only hitching a ride." Bishop knocked the tool from the engineer's grasp, with a gunbarrel. It fell out of the cab. "Kindly put the spurs to this coal-eater . . . we want more speed! Ballinger! Where the hell — oh, there you are. Can you run this thing?"

"Sure!" Banjo Ballinger came climbing over the tender behind the locomotive. Taking the scoop from the fireman, he fed coal into the firebox. "I ran a narrow-gauge dinky once for a mining company. Nothing to it."

Bishop ran his eyes over the array of polished levers. He knew nothing whatever of railroading, except that sometimes it was an intrusive nuisance. Machinery he abhorred. He put his faith altogether into his hands and wits. Nimble hands. Shrewd wits, scoundrelly clever, but baffled by the mysteries of mechanics.

"Which one of these doodads do you wiggle to fetch up a gallop? I don't see any labels on 'em."

"The throttle, Bishop — the throttle!" Leaving his work at the glowing, refueled firebox, Banjo shoved the stuttering engineer aside. "This is it, I guess. Yeah, see? Just yank it open." He illustrated his superior knowledge. "Like this." The train jolted, lunging forward. "Simple, driving these things. Any fool could do it."

The engineer uttered an outraged bellow at the slur on his prideful profession. "The hell! Quit it, you crazy idiots! My train has got to stop this side o' Trinidad an' ease in after daylight! Special orders! Shipment of wild cattle waiting in the loading pens! Order says don't upset 'em!"

"Skipper," said Banjo, "you don't know those cattle like I do. They're my cows. Your train won't upset 'em. It'll explode 'em! More speed, Mr. Bishop?"

"Throw on the coal!" Bishop tugged the throttle wide open. "Where's the whistle?"

"That cord there over your head, on the left, I think. The other one, on your right, is probably the bell."

"We'll pull both, to make sure." Bishop did so. Above the resulting raucous racket, he called, "Any idea where Rico is?"

"He jumped on the tail-end, him and his cutthroat gang," Banjo answered, shoveling coal. "They're riding the bumps. They won't make it up here on the catwalks. It'd take a monkey, the way this train rides!"

"Pretty rough."

"Rough? This roadbed's murder! Listen to us hitting the tracks, screeching and bucking on every bump. These things ain't perfect yet by a long shot. I'll take a good horse for mine," said Banjo as he fed the firebox.

"Me too."

"Sure. You can go to sleep on a horse, a good horse, and it'll get you home. They've got savvy. Doze off on this iron whoozis, you're liable to end anywhere. Right, Skipper?" he addressed the engineer companionably.

The engineer refrained from voicing his opinion. He and the fireman huddled at the right-hand door of the cab, trying to decide whether to jump out or wait for the worst. The rest of the train crew must have already jumped off, none putting in an appearance to inquire the wherefore of the maniacal speed in a crawl-safe zone, probably thinking the engineer had gone mad.

"Those critters'll stompede from here to Pikes Peak!" Banjo predicted.

The train screeched around shallow curves, lurching perilously, steel grinding on steel. On the straight stretches it hit a speed never contemplated by its designers. On the last curve of the downgrade the inside wheels lifted, pounding the rail. The cab shivered. The slam and bang of the cattle cars sounded like collisions, one after another, as they whipped past the curve.

The fireman shut his eyes tight, praying loudly. He was apparently a Mormon convert with an unregenerate Presbyterian holdover, possibly lowland Scottish or Ulster Irish, judging from the shape and accent of his prayers. The engineer just stared out, stricken dumb, eyes as big as silver dollars.

The lights of Trinidad came rushing to meet the empty cattle train as if in welcome to its arrival. A new railhead, a Johnny-come-lately boomtown, Trinidad stood ready to feed and buy drinks for the train crew. Trinidad didn't yet suspect what was coming.

Bishop took a fresh bite on his cigar, a Mexican brand of cigar that he favored, long and black as a New England cheroot. Banjo Ballinger, snatching time out from stoking, rolled and lit a brown cigarette. They gazed interestedly ahead.

Wheels pounding, whistle hooting and bell clanging, sparks streaming from the smokestack, the train hurtled into Trinidad, Colorado, just north of New Mexico.

8

Under the single glaring headlight of the locomotive, the loading chutes of the railroad pens jutted up aslant like gangways leading to nowhere. By day, when loading into cattle cars, the chutes were a turmoil — steers bawling, punchers sweatily prodding them up into the cars, tally men scribbling fast and cursing . . .

This was night, dark, time for uneasy repose if any Arizona cow knew the meaning of repose — doubtful, since they were cactus-busters, distrustful, wild as deer and dangerous as bears with cubs. They'd charge a man on horseback. A man afoot they'd hook to bloody smithereens.

A multitude of long horns and red eyes, shining, sprouted up from the railroad pens. For an instant the cattle stayed motionless, fear-frozen by the blinding glare and the clangor of the onrushing monster.

Panic struck. The great ungainly bodies

reared hump-backed, stiff-tailed. The snorting bawl was a screaming blare that no cattleman could mistake for anything else than a mad stampede. Pawing, kicking, the steers piled up against the fences enclosing them, all trying to climb over their brethren, to get free of the railroad pens and away from the terror.

A fence crumpled. The sound of it made only a splintering crackle, a puny sound under the loud clash of clacking bones, horns and hoofs. Then another fence. And another.

The railroad pens had been built to contain reasonably belligerent cattle. They couldn't withstand the jar of the Banjo brand. The animals broke loose.

"There they go!" said Bishop.

The dark shapes charged free from the broken pens, heads thrust forward like double-pronged battering rams. The matter of a town standing in their way, with its people, raised small obstruction to their frantic flight.

"They're off!" Bishop said, satisfied with a task well done. The first part of the task, anyway. Already, the town was in an uproar, citizens fleeing to shelter, cursing the train and bedamning the railroad — the A.T.&S.F. — that had brought prosperity to

Trinidad. No so-called soulless corporation could expect gratitude; it didn't make a mark on the profit side of the ledger.

Besides, anyone out on the streets at this time of night, man or woman, was up to no good.

The rest of the task depended upon ensuing events. As a wryly cynical optimist, Bishop leaned strongly toward bending circumstances to make them fit his own design, more or less. He shut off the throttle. The train coasted on, no slackening of speed, roaring through town.

"How d'you halt this goddam thing, Ballinger? We've got to get off now!"

"The brake!" Banjo pulled his head in from peering at the mainstreet, where belligerent steers chased humans. "Where's the brake?"

"How the hell do I know? You said you know how to run a train!"

"I ran it, didn't I? Stopping it — I dunno, it's rigged different than the dinky I ran down in —"

"Damn you and your dinky, you don't know any more about this rattle-chariot than I do! Hey, engineer! Where's the brake? Tell me what to pull, or I'll buffalo you!"

The engineer gabbled something about the risk of wrecking the train, throwing on the emergency brake at this speed. Then he changed his tune, something worse occurring to him, and he yelled for the emergency brake. He and his fireman tensed to leap out of the cab.

"This, you mean — or this?" Banjo shouted. He tugged at every lever.

Common prudence told Bishop to take a fast grip on the handrail, the nearest firm object at hand. Even so, the next moment he came within an inch of cracking his front teeth. Banjo had got results, more than he'd anticipated.

The flanged wheels of the engine, suddenly locked tight by brakes, shrieked, gouging the rails. Bishop, thrown forward, saved his teeth by the strength of his arms. The train abruptly lost its momentum in a series of violent jerks that flung forward everything loose, the string of cattle cars crashing behind the skidding locomotive and forcing it on.

The engineer and the fireman, foreseeing disaster to the train, took their chance to leap out from the lurching cab.

Bishop, too, braced ready to jump out. The train was screeching past his destination — Doc Sunday's Livery — where, he hoped, forty thousand dollars was hidden. A good bundle of plunder, well worth the time and risk.

At the back of his mind itched a thought that he might be wrong. Money, big money, had lured many straight gunfighters away from their code, made them gunmen, killers. So far, he had respected the code. Give the other man an even break. Help him up if he's down. Plain law of the range, unwritten but ever recognized, like the law demanding that a rider take care of his horse before himself.

Bishop looked around to see what was delaying Banjo Ballinger's exit from the cab, and saw the reason. Banjo lay conked out, evidently having fetched his head a stunning crack against something or other when the train first bucked on locked wheels.

Coughing up the cigar that the edge of the cab had rammed past his teeth, Bishop swore and bent over the unconscious young Arizonian, trying to shake him to his senses. But Banjo didn't even groan, out cold, dead to the world, his forehead bloodily bruised.

The train shivered, slowing to a crawl. Back along the tracks, the train crew, running after it, howled for help from the town. The town, however, had more than it could cope with, wild steers charging through its streets.

Bishop swore again, abandoning his efforts to bring Banjo to life. The situation exasperated him. Here was his golden opportunity to ransack Doc Sunday's quarters while Trinidad was chaotic. And here this unlucky cowman had to get himself knocked senseless, at the most critical time.

He couldn't let Banjo fall victim to the wrathy vengeance of the pursuing train crew and the towners. The guy was a sort of partner. Yet lugging him along was out of the question. Bishop debated the problem and reached a decision that struck him as a fair and reasonable compromise.

"Best I can do for you, feller, is run you clear out," he muttered. "The rest is up to you, when you wake up."

He located the locked emergency brake and released it, then opened the throttle and jumped down out of the cab. The train's slowing roll picked up speedily, a full head of steam in the boiler.

The string of cattle cars rumbled past Bishop, steadily increasing speed, leaving the chasing train crew far behind. He reasoned that the train would trundle on until Banjo Ballinger woke up in safety and stopped it, somewhere along the line. By then Banjo would be pretty well out of danger. As to what his difficulties might be afterward — well, that was his affair. No man had a right to expect too much from getting himself buffaloed by an engine.

He cut toward Doc Sunday's Livery. Seeing no sign of Don Ricardo and the *guerrero* squad, who must have quit the train minutes ago when it slowed down, he muttered oaths on the banged head of Banjo Ballinger. While he'd spent precious time on Banjo, the don most likely had rapidly raided Doc Sunday's quarters and got away with the forty thousand dollars, damn him.

Trinidad was in turmoil, overrun by two thousand head of rampaging longhorns that didn't know a street from a gully. Bishop dodged two belligerent steers, ducked into an alley off the plaza, and set his course at a rough guess from there to his proposed destination.

A terrific crash rang out from south of town. It boomed into the night, dwarfing all other sounds. It came from down along the railroad right-of-way, the fearful smash of a speeding train at the end of rails, wrecking itself. Bishop had clean forgotten that the tracks weren't finished. That accounted for the worry of the engineer and the fireman, he guessed. They had foreseen the smash-up. A pity they didn't mention it before jumping off the doomed train. A neglectful oversight, caused by the urgent stress of the moment.

Bishop shook his head, sorry for Banjo Ballinger in the cab of the wrecked locomotive. That Arizonian had met misfortune ever since arriving in Trinidad. Bad luck dogged him. Some men seemed fated, at times, to suffer a rash of disasters. Bishop had weathered through such malignant periods, when nothing went right, stray accidents ruining plans.

By the look of things, most of the Banjo-brand herd had already stampeded through Trinidad and charged on out into open country, leaving devastation and shattered nerves behind to mark their hurricane passing. A few bawling steers still roamed the streets, but the tumultuous uproar of the town was subsiding.

Bishop slipped around to the rear of Doc Sunday's Livery Stable — Best in the West. He had a foreboding that his delay in getting off the runaway train had lost him the trick. Success of the trick had depended upon instant timing and fast action. As a cover, a diversion, the stampede could be counted on for only a brief period.

As soon as he stared in through Doc Sunday's rear door, he knew for a cold fact that he was too late. Don Ricardo de Risa and his ruffians had also passed through and left their mark, ahead of him. There wasn't a horse left in the livery stable. Among the missing horses was Bishop's own big black, leaving Bishop afoot and too blazing mad to swear.

The don had turned the trick on him — jumped off the train, promptly raided the livery, and apparently got clear. A fast job, even faster than according to plan, Bishop's plan. What more had the don captured, Bishop wondered grittily, besides the horses? The money, too?

"Goddam twister!"

Out in the street, in front of the livery, a group of dazed townsmen pelted questions at a shaken stableman.

"What hit this place, Harvey? I saw some Mexicans run in, then ride out —"

"Who was they? I saw 'em, but the cows —"

"Where's —"

The stableman, finding his voice, made himself heard with a shout. "Cut the squallin' an' I'll tell you! It was the Risa mob. They took the horses after they broke into Doc's office."

"You mean the horses busted into —"

105

"No! The cows come stompedin' from the pens, see? Vada Conant runs in here off the street. I ask her to bolt the doors while I go to the horses — they was huffy at the noise. The Risa mob pushed in that minute. They searched Doc's office. Then they grabbed Vada."

"They *wha-aat?* Does Marshal Conant know?"

"He sure does!" said the stableman. "Vada let out a screech that brung Conant runnin' in. He tried to fight, but it was no go. They buff'loed him. Nothin' I could do — I was backed up to the wall with a gun in my face. That Risa bandit, he came out o' Doc's office cussin' soft an' low. He gave 'em orders. They saddled up the horses, slung Conant on one, Vada on another, an' took off."

"Took the marshal *and* his daughter? Jeeze-creest! We want a posse! Where's Conant's deputies? Where's Doc Sunday?"

"Far's I know," the stableman answered, "the deputies went on the trail of the Risa gang, after the Casa Colorado break-out. They sure missed! Maybe they stopped for a drink on the way. Doc left for his ranch. Told me he'd be back soon. He's gonna be damn sore 'bout this. Most likely he heard the noise. But this ain't no fault o' mine. I ain't no fightin' man. Just a common

106

ord'n'ry —"

Someone in the street group interrupted his plaintive confession of cowardice. "There's Doc Sunday's buckboard coming now! Man, oh, man, look at that team run! He heard the noise, all right, Harvey!"

Bishop eased on through the stable. In the dim light of a single lantern it showed the results of Don Ricardo's swift raid, nothing left but the feed boxes, bits of horse gear, and Doc Sunday's medicine cabinet containing bottles, jars, and his old metal box labeled imposingly PRESCRIPTIONS. He trod to the front entrance and risked peering out into the street.

The group was hastily splitting apart to make way for an oncoming buckboard drawn by a fine pair of dun racers. Doc Sunday, driving without any regard for the townsmen's safety, swerved in and reined the team to a halt squarely in front of his livery stable, at the foot of the ramp. He stood up in the buckboard. He was small, skinny, a shrunken wisp of an old man in stingily genteel attire, yet he frowned about him with an air of despotic command. And the group fell silent under the frown of that shabby little man, fearing his displeasure, as if he wielded the power of life and death.

"Who let my cattle loose? What's going on

here behind my back?" Even his reedy voice held dominance and threat. "Where are you, Tate?"

It was incongruous to see Shang Tate, roughneck gunman, deputy marshal, shuffle forward like a culprit going before a hanging judge. Wherever Conant's deputies had gone, Shang Tate hadn't gone with them, possibly because of bruises received from Bishop's boot.

"The Risa crew came back on a cattle train, Doc," he reported, his manner a mixture of sullen defensiveness and uneasy servility. "Nobody was expecting 'em. They stompeded your cows, which sent us all to cover. In the stompede they raided the livery an' your office. They caught Conant an' his daughter, 'cording to Harvey, an' got away!"

Doc Sunday stood very still. Only his sucked-in lips, bloodless, papery crinkled, betrayed his emotions at the news. Rigidly self-controlled from leading what amounted to a double life, he didn't rant and curse, nor hurl blame at anyone.

"Get after them!" he said. "Form up a posse!"

"How?" Shang Tate asked. "Them steers came through too fast for anybody to reach a hitching rack. The horses hightailed. All's left of 'em is busted bridle reins. An' the

Risa crew took every horse in your stable. If there's any horses left in town, 'cept your team . . . Hell's pitchpot, what's a-coming now?"

Coming up the street was the train crew, bawling for the law, dragging a banged-up young Arizona cowman in their midst, who, half senseless, wagged his bloodied head bewilderedly at the sad fate that had befallen him.

"He wrecked my train!" the engineer bellowed at the group of men in front of the livery stable. He seemed to hold them responsible, or all of Trinidad. "Him and a big blackguard, they took my train an' wrecked it off the rails! You got law here? Where's the jail? My train . . ."

The group of men shifted, surrounding the trainmen and their sagging captive. Shang Tate called tonelessly to Doc Sunday, "It's Ballinger, dam'f it ain't! Want me to gun him?"

9

Bishop flipped up a gun from under his black coat as he headed out of the livery stable. He knocked down two men in his exit, and leaped onto the buckboard. It was the only getaway left to him; be damned if he'd run on foot like a thief in the night.

He had compromised many times, in the past, with his code of self-respect. Too many times. The shining shield was badly tarnished. A man had to live, had to make his bargain with life. Especially a notorious gunfighter. He was like Don Ricardo, in the same kettle — trying to stay decent, halfway or thereabouts, all odds against it . . .

Doc Sunday didn't have time to be more than startled and no time at all in which to do anything about it. The buckboard bounced on its springs as Bishop landed on it, and Doc Sunday, almost losing his standing balance, whirled around. A large and ungentle hand crammed his plug hat down over his eyes. Doc Sunday whooshed an oath, never so affronted in a long while. He sank. A foot, well booted, planted itself on him and held him there on the floorboards securely out of mischief.

Bishop then snatched up the lines and slapped them hard down along the backs of the team. The pair of duns lunged forward in obedience, scattering once more the group of townsmen, who had gathered around the angry train crew.

What the group thought of that was contained in a medley of astounded yells. Bishop chopped a hastily parting shot at Shang Tate, in payment for the buck-toothed gunman's proposal to kill Ballinger, but Tate, dodging alertly behind the engineer, was already trying to get off a shot on his own account.

The engineer, leery of being placed in a crossfire, skipped aside and jostled Tate's aim. The last Bishop saw of them, they were sidestepping each other like a couple of clumsy dancers. Others of the group began shooting when they realized what had happened — that Doc Sunday was being actually kidnaped, buckboard and all — but by that time the fast duns were running in full stride.

The buckboard careened around a bend

on two wheels and jounced out of the street's dried ruts. Bishop reined the duns southward to the Taos Trail, same old trail scored in the earth for half a century by the traders' wagons, now followed by the railroad. He judged that Don Ricardo de Risa would have cut south after his raid, with his two captives.

Trinidad was as far north as Don Ricardo had ever operated, to Bishop's knowledge. Long way from home. Rich temptation must have lured him way up here into Colorado: the profit of stolen cattle and horses — Doc Sunday the ready-cash market. Yes.

But the don must have established a hidden headquarters somewhere, to fall back on. He wasn't a fool, for all his reckless daring. Not by any means. His headquarters must be somewhere to the south, most likely across the line in New Mexico where nobody answered straight questions straightly nor told of what they knew and had seen — New Mexicans having come only lately under the U.S. flag, perforce, and nursing meager love for the intrusive gringo.

Bishop, long legs straddled, took his booted foot off Doc Sunday, who lay joggling on the bouncing floor of the buckboard. The duns raced like tireless greyhounds, requiring most of his attention as well as his balance. "If you know where de Risa camps — and I guess you do know —" he began, then found he had to remedy a mistake.

Doc Sunday, released, plucked out a snubby pistol while scrambling up from the floorboards. Quick as a darting lizard, he jabbed it at his tall captor.

Bishop struck at the derringer. It exploded its single load, searing his forearm, ripping the sleeve of his black coat from cuff to elbow. He grabbed hold of it, tore it from Doc Sunday's hand, and in wrath he flung it away overside. With one hand he hauled Doc Sunday onto his feet, shook him, plumped him into the spring seat.

"Take the lines! Sit there and drive, you goddam wasp, I'm right behind you! Drive to de Risa's camp!"

"I don't know where it is!" Doc Sunday whined.

"Liar!" Bishop blasted at him. "You must know! You've been hand-in-glove with him on deals — stolen stock, cattle and horses, holdups . . . You know where to find de Risa when you want him. Drive there!"

"Very well. Do my best . . ."

Doc Sunday wasn't yet at the end of his

tether, not by a long stretch. There coiled darkly dangerous depths in him, depths of hate, vitriolic viciousness, masked behind the mild and shabbily genteel appearance.

When Bishop turned his head to gaze rearward for possible pursuers, Doc Sunday stooped and straightened up again so swiftly that Bishop, catching the movement out of the corner of his eye, ducked barely in time for Doc's black veterinary bag to sail inches over his head. Before the bag landed in the brush that lined the trail, Bishop had his fingers clasped on Doc Sunday's scrawny neck.

"One more bit of horseplay, and I'll use you for a quirt!" he growled. Menacing gray eyes stared into baleful green eyes. "Drive me to de Risa's hole-up, hear? If I don't see it tonight, you won't see sunup in the morning! That's a promise. You bear it in mind! I'd as soon shoot you as I'd shoot an old rattler at my feet!"

"I'm sure you would, Mr. Bishop! As a gunman —"

"Gunfighter, please!"

"Excuse me! Merely a difference in terminology. Rather hair-splitting. You *do* live by your proficiency with your guns, Mr. Bishop, don't you?"

Bishop didn't reply.

■ ■ ■ ■

In the graying dawn Doc Sunday drew the team to a halt. An hour ago he had turned off from the main roadway of the Santa Fe Trail, onto a little-used track that meandered through a dense growth of dwarf piñon and juniper. The duns snuffled, weary and discontented, needing water.

He sat slumped, the lines loosening in his fingers, his face parchment-pale, all vitality drained from it. "An old Pueblo Indian mission," he muttered in a dry whisper. "Adobe. Long ago abandoned, forgotten. It's about a mile farther on."

"De Risa's hideout?"

"Yes. He and his men . . . Since last spring. They use it to hold stolen stock. I bought from them. Cattle and horses. They may have gone back there. Maybe not. I don't know. It's a — it's a stronghold. High walls. Thick. They mended the breaks."

"You did more'n buy their stolen stock! You planned their holdups, on percentage! And finally double-crossed 'em, on the Ballinger haul! Grasping old devil, you stretched too far that time! Nobody hooks de Risa and gets away with it. Nobody," Bishop amended, "except me, sometimes.

115

Just sometimes. Only because I know him pretty well."

He thought fleetingly of the many times he and Don Ricardo de Risa had clashed. One day, he supposed, they would shoot it out. Both would die, for they were matched so close, within a hair's breadth of draw-and-trigger. End of a feud. Yet, curiously, they liked each other. Between them was real respect, a feeling akin to brotherhood.

Doc Sunday twisted his head slowly to Bishop, while the halted duns sniffed contemptuously at the sparse dry grass. The fear in his eyes showed naked and ugly; a dread of pain. This shriveled old man possessed brains, nerve, self-control, but he was drawn too tight now. His kind of bravery could be broken, under the pressure of direct stress.

"Let me go!" he whispered. His lower lip, caked with dried skin, trembled as if he was about to burst out sobbing like a maudlin drunkard. "If they get hold of me — after what I . . . Oh, God! They'll skin me alive!"

Bishop was not incapable of pity, but he hadn't much of it to spare for this viperish old devil. Hypocrisy was a cardinal sin in his book. "Drive on!" he commanded.

Doc Sunday shut his eyes, shaking his head. Reaching over him, Bishop shook the lines and got the team started up again. He looked forward to catching up with Don Ricardo. What would happen when he did, he hadn't any clear idea. This thing had to be played as he went along, step by slippery step.

"Is that the place?" he inquired presently. Huge walls, immensely thick, loomed high as the buckboard rolled onward.

"That's it!"

"H'm. I see what you mean. Looks grim."

The old mission had obviously served also as a Pueblo stronghold, for protection from the marauding Comanches and Apaches whose sport for long ages had been to raid the less warlike Pueblo tribes. The bases of its walls, built of rock and *caliche,* supported the remnants of adobe battlements, broken and eroded.

Once a swarming beehive of activity, now it stood abandoned and forgotten, crumbling bit by bit with the passing years. It had outlived its time and its usefulness, and been left to join the lonely company of other ruins of its kind, for the heyday of Spanish-sponsored missions was gone forever. What had been a *kiva* was merely a deep hole in the earth, its underground ceremonial chamber choked with the rubble of its collapsed roof. In their day, Spanish mission-ary monks had learned to make allowance for the ancient traditions of their Indian converts and not to pry into *kiva* mysteries.

Bishop, not trusting the silence of the place, drew in the duns. There were many hoofprints in the bare expanse of hard earth. Ahead gaped the gateway through the wall, wide open, nothing left of what must once have been a massive wooden gate and beamed frame. He dropped down off the halted buckboard and ducked partly behind it, his eyes fixed on the ruined *kiva.* He had an impression of slight and sly movement there in that hole.

"Get down!" he told Doc Sunday. "Quick!"

The movement in the hole became posi-tive, became a poking carbine. Its barrel twinkled a reflection briefly from the sun. He was not startled when it cracked an echoing report into the stillness. He wished he had a rifle, to pay back that sniper. The distance was somewhat too far for accurate six-gun shooting. He would not waste his shells.

The bullet from the carbine hissed over-head, very near Doc Sunday who, bursting from his petrified fright, scrambled out of the buckboard. Again the carbine spanged, this time lower, the bullet smashing through the low sideboard and ripping the leather-padded seat. The duns stamped hoofs. The carbine shooter was having sport, dangerous sport calculated to impress upon Bishop the fact that he was within range and without cover.

Bishop sent forward a hail. "Rico! You better call off that *carbinero.*"

"Why?" came the question from behind the walls.

"He might hit Doc Sunday, here."

"So?"

"You didn't find the money, or you wouldn't have carried off Conant and his daughter. Not Conant, anyway. I didn't find it, either. So Doc's still the only one who knows where to lay hand on it."

He waited for that to sink in. No further shots cracked from the *kiva.* Somewhere up the Sangre de Cristo slopes two coyotes exchanged morning howls, thin and wavering, and silence crept back. The sun blazed aslant from the cloudless blue sky. Another hot day, barely saved from scorching by the altitude. Far down in the desert lowlands the heat would be cruel.

Perhaps that was the reason Rico had made camp here, rather than push on south and risk ruining the horses. It was possible that he had actually found the money, and had carried off Conant and his daughter as hostages in case strong pursuit crowded him. Perhaps, Bishop reflected, I'm making an empty bluff, and he's laughing at me.

"Come on in!" Don Ricardo called. "Bring your scraggy little friend with you!"

"The hell with that!" Bishop countered. "You come out and we'll talk things over. Or have you sunk into skulking habits like a bushwhacking badman?" he queried. Under his breath he muttered, "That ought to fetch him!"

It did. Don Ricardo de Risa appeared at the shadowy big gateway, emerging into the bright morning sunlight. After him slouched five of his *guerreros,* carbines pointed at the ready and fingers on the triggers.

"Here we go!" Bishop muttered.

He stepped clear of the buckboard and team. He spread his coat open, and made no bones about putting the palms of his hands preparedly on the smooth butts of his holstered guns. A warning. A kind of courtesy, like the oldtime sword salute to an adversary before a duel.

10

The dapper don paced stiffly as a fighting cock, his sombrero tilted to shade his eyes from the sun. The white bone butts of his guns rocked jerkily in their silver-studded holsters, tied snug and low to his thighs. In response to Bishop's gesture, he matched it by resting his hands on them. A finger of one hand flashed a diamond. More than once in his career he had been wealthy, even influential politically. Expensive tastes had squandered the fortunes. A restlessly volatile temperament had led to intrigues, disgrace, flight. An incorrigible scoundrel. Enemy of authority. Outlaw.

He was halfway across the stretch of barren ground between the ancient mission-stronghold and the buckboard, when Bishop's voice, weighted with warning, stopped him.

"Leave your men there!"

Don Ricardo hesitated, figuring chances,

and Bishop asked him bitingly, "Must you have five guns backing you against me? I've seen the day when you had more nerve — a hell-sight more! Are you slipping?"

Stung where it hurt worst, the don drew himself so rigidly erect that he trembled slightly. The slur cut deep. Any gunfighter hated the thought of loss of steel nerve, feared it. He snapped a word that halted the five armed men behind him, and advanced alone.

"A pleasure to see you, Rogue!"

He conjured up a smile, meant to be bland. Then, the effort restoring his self-possession, he stood quietly alert. His saving grace, as a bloody bandit, was polite courtesy. He still retained a few principles — of behavior, not of action.

"I worried that some misfortune might have befallen you in Trinidad," he said in his meticulous and somewhat quaintly stilted English.

He claimed to have studied at Oxford in his youth. Maybe he had, as the offspring of a rich Spanish family. Maybe not. He was a barefaced liar from the cradle. A born crook. You couldn't believe anything he said.

"What delayed you, Rogue, coming here?"

"A goddam thief stole my horse from the livery!"

"How fortunate that you were able to secure another means of conveyance — and its owner, too!" The dark eyes touched frigidly on Doc Sunday.

Doc Sunday cringed, his creased face blanched white. He had double-crossed Don Ricardo de Risa, cheated him out of the holdup loot, Ballinger's forty thousand dollars, believing he was safe. Now the reckoning, which he hadn't foreseen. The vengeance, robber's vengeance on a betrayer . . .

"Very fortunate," Bishop agreed, "seeing I was left afoot. You didn't leave any horses handy in town."

"An oversight for which I apologize," said the don blandly. "I'm sorry it inconvenienced you, Rogue." He had never been sorry for any trick he could pull on Bishop, and wasn't now. Far from it. And Bishop knew it. "Ballinger?"

"Ballinger met up with a mishap — a train wreck. He's in the Trinidad jail."

"*Que lastima!* That unlucky young man . . . But I am remiss in my duties as host. You must be thirsty. Coffee? A drink? I have some tequilla, Oso Negro. Your favorite brand, if I remember correctly. Black Bear. Right?"

Bishop nodded his head consideringly.

Any day that didn't begin with black coffee, strongly fortified with a lacing of spirits and a full shot glass on the side, was a bad day for him. He wasn't a drunkard by any means; had never got drunk in his life. He simply had the masculine vices of a confirmed bachelor, a loner. Drank too much smoked too much — to hell with it, life was short, meant to be enjoyed while it lasted. That summed up his pagan philosophy, right or wrong.

"Bring out the coffee and tequila, Rico!"

"In the old mission —"

"No! Out here!"

Don Ricardo cast a glance back at his five followers, then again at the tall, flinty-faced gunfighter confronting him. A word or gesture from him could spark an explosion — but no profit from it, no satisfaction from dying in the blow-up. Don Ricardo was well acquainted, from past observation, with Bishop's pair of long-barreled guns, their deadly swiftness in the hands of a master. He nursed a healthy respect for them, as well as a reluctant and half-mocking regard for the man who wore them.

"No coffee, then. No drink. No water for your team, nor grain — of which we have plenty stored. What do you want?"

"I'm here to make a trade with you."

"*Bueno!* I'll trade you your horse, saddle and all, for Doc Sunday."

"Not good enough, Rico. Raise it." The fact that Don Ricardo wanted Doc Sunday, squirming in his hands, convinced Bishop that he wasn't making an empty bluff. The don had tipped his cards, unwittingly. He never had played good poker.

"You missed getting hold of Ballinger's forty thousand dollars, same as me," Bishop said. "Doc's the key to it, and I've got him! I could put a bullet through his head, and there goes the key! Is that plain?"

"Yes. What do you propose?"

"I propose you bring out your hostages, particularly Conant's daughter, unharmed. Then we'll get down to business. Not before!"

"I give you my oath —"

"I wouldn't take your oath on a mountain of Bibles, you tricky cuss!"

Don Ricardo shrugged his shoulders high, Spanish fashion, meantime keenly watching Bishop's splayed hands. At last he turned and spoke crisply, and one of the five followers trotted back into the old mission.

Soon, Marshal Tom Conant and Vada appeared, walking, escorted by the remainder of the don's full force, heavily armed *hombres del campo,* veteran bandits who didn't expect to die of old age. The don spoke again. Conant was brought forward alone, leaving the girl at the midway point surrounded by hairy faces and the smell of long-unwashed exiles from their southern homeland. It was dry country.

Haggard, his head bandaged with a rag, Marshal Conant plodded stumblingly forward under the rough nudges of the guards. He sighted Doc Sunday. His grayed face twitched into an expression of futile rage.

"Hell burn you, Doc!" he burst out. "Look what you've done to me — to my daughter! I've strung along, played it your way, done dirty work . . . But I warned you! I warned you never to drag Vada into the sorry mess!"

To Bishop, the town marshal said in an aside, in simple explanation, "My wife is an invalid, bedridden. I have to do what I can . . ."

"Sure," said Bishop comfortingly. He had never yet married, never would.

He distrusted women. They flocked around him in the bars and dance halls, sensing his powerful virility, and he enjoyed them. But marriage, a settled life, no. He wasn't cut out for it. *Gather ye roses while ye may . . .*

"Shut up!" Doc Sunday snarled at Conant. "Shut your mouth, you damned fool!"

Don Ricardo winked to Bishop. "When thieves fall out! Keep talking, Conant — confession is good for the soul! Or so I was told in my innocent youth."

"You never were innocent!" Bishop growled. "Devil's whelp from the day you were born!"

"We're two of a kind!"

"Yeah, guess we are, Rico. Guess we are. Two of a kind." The lost dreams of youth. Splendid ambitions gone down the drain. Life was too tough for tender young dreams, if he'd had them.

Marshal Tom Conant pointed a rigid forefinger at Doc Sunday. "He blackmailed me. I made a slip when I was a youngster up in Montana. It threw me in with a wild bunch for a while. He knew about it. Held it over me. It was long ago, but . . . Oh, I'm not excusing myself, 'cept I've had my wife and daughter to think of. My position in Trinidad. All that."

"So you knuckled under to him," Bishop commented. He had known of it in other places and times. The first surrender was the fatal step. "Did him special favors, eh?"

"At first they were small favors, things that didn't hurt anybody much. They got bigger, till I was in too deep to back out. Till I was taking his private orders. My deputies were picked by him. His crew. I only pass his orders on to them. My own say-so don't count any more. That's how far down I've sunk. But now I've had enough! I'm through!"

"What do you want to do?" Don Ricardo asked.

"I want to get out of the sorry mess with my wife and daughter safe."

"You know a good deal about Doc Sunday's secrets, don't you, Conant?"

"Too much!"

"Would you be willing to agree to expose him? Publicly in Trinidad, telling all you know?"

Bishop cut a rapid glance at the don, recognizing that he was leading up to one of his tricks, and not liking it. Doc Sunday started to speak, but put a hand to his mouth as if he feared a blow.

Conant looked taken aback at the unexpected question. "That's tough to answer," he said. "For one thing, if I was to publicly expose Doc for what he is, it'd mean I'd have to do the same to myself, wouldn't it?"

"True. It would all come out."

"Trinidad folks are complaining. Too many crimes and nobody arrested. Holdups.

128

Trail drivers robbed. There's those who're saying — they don't say it out loud as yet — that maybe I'm in cahoots with whoever's behind the robberies."

"Which also is true!"

"I don't deny it, not to you, Risa. But if I was to spill the works in Trinidad — tell it all . . ." Shaking his head, Conant showed nakedly the weak streak that flawed his character. "I couldn't face it!"

Don Ricardo de Risa shrugged. "If you can't agree to do it, then you can't have your daughter! That's the price!" Eyes purposely merciless, he said, "She goes to Mexico with me! When I'm tired of her, I'll sell her to the highest bidder, probably to Yaquis who like the color of her hair."

He was running a bluff, Bishop thought — hoped. He hadn't been crude and coarse in the old days. Still, one could never tell, never foresee the result of rough and desperate years on an outlaw. Brutality bred worse brutality as a matter of course, it was cumulative like an avalanche, one hurtling rock dislodging a dozen more downward.

Conant, of course, didn't think the don's wickedly worded threat was a bluff. In any case, he wouldn't call it, his own daughter, only child, being at stake. He clenched his fists tight, gray face twitching uncontrollably, restraining his urge to smash the don in the face.

"I agree to do it!" he husked finally.

Don Ricardo, sure in advance of the answer, already had shifted his attention to Doc Sunday. "And you, old monkey! What price do you pay, to keep me from making Conant betray you? Shall we say forty thousand dollars? Ballinger's goldbacks?"

Now the trick fell into shape and made sense. A squeeze play. Doc Sunday's thin, dry lips sucked in. "I'll write you out a check, de Risa." Even then, in extremity, in fear for his very life, he could still make an attempt to guard his gains. The forlorn attempt of a miser.

"You'll give me the cash!"

"It's in the bank . . ."

"Liar!" snapped the don. "You wouldn't have dared to bank so much stolen money! You hid it. My patience is wearing thin, I warn you! I will have that money, or you will roast over a slow fire! Till your eyeballs pop from their sockets and your skinny flesh —"

"All right, you can have the money!"

Don Ricardo's white teeth bared in a smile. "I'll have it! Conant, you go with him. Get it from him! Your daughter will be free when you deliver it to me, not a minute before!"

"What if there's a slip-up?" Conant protested. "I'll do my best, God knows, but something might happen to stop me from —"

"Let nothing stop you! I'll not make any allowance for failure! You'll have your gun. Stay close to Doc until he hands you the money."

"Then do I bring it way down here to you?"

The don shook his head. "Too far, too risky. Once you left town, Doc would send the crew of deputies fast after you."

"That's what I was thinking," Conant said. "They'd cut me down and bury me lonely, like they've done others, on his order. So how do I get the money to you?"

Bishop gave thought to that, too. Don Ricardo couldn't risk another foray into Trinidad with his depleted band, even if he could persuade the *guerreros* to try it. They'd be cut to pieces. On the other hand, Conant would be marked for death by the deputies if he left town carrying Doc Sunday's loot.

Not surprisingly, the don had a solution to the problem. His fertile brain was seldom at a loss.

"You and Doc will use the buckboard, Conant," he said. "I and my men will follow at a distance, part of the way. If Doc tries anything on you, we'll skin him alive."

After the dire threat of roasting over a slow fire, skinning alive lost by comparison some of its horror. Realizing it, he appended, "And then we'll bury him in an ant hill."

He turned back to Conant. "When you have the money, lie low until sundown, then ride north out of Trinidad. Be sure you have a good horse ready. Tie up the money in a sack to your saddle, because you'll be riding hard."

Conant nodded. "At sundown I make a fast bolt."

"North," Don Ricardo reminded him. "And stay on the road out. We'll be there to cover your getaway. You won't see us, but the deputies chasing you —"

"You'll ambush 'em!"

"*'Buscado!* We have a score to settle with that crew, anyway."

"And if I get clear?"

"You ride on then to that gravel pit up along the railroad line, between the road and the rails. The gravel pit that the graders used, building the railroad bed. You know the place?"

"Do I! Those Irish pick-an'-shovel stiffs! They raised more hell —"

"You halt there and wait for us," commanded the don. "It is deserted now. Be there with the money when we arrive — or bid your daughter farewell forever! Get started!"

"Hold it a minute!" Bishop put in. They all looked at him. "A neat set-up, Rico!" he rasped. "It could go right, or it could go wrong — but what's in it for me?"

He had his black coat spread open. His thumbs rested on the upper edges of displayed gun belts, fingers fanned below. He knew that the don was aware of the potential significance of that stance, the bare threat of it. The don was fast, deadly fast. The don claimed correctly that he could outdraw any man he had met except one. The exception was Bishop, and the don didn't pretend otherwise.

"Your magnificent black horse, *amigo* . . . Which you value highly, rightly so. It is in my possession. I would grieve to part with it, but —"

"That's not enough! My stake in this caper amounts to more than a horse — my own horse, at that!"

11

Don Ricardo de Risa eyed those muscular, flexible hands. Trained hands of a master cardsharp, of an ace gunfighter and free-lance troubleshooter. Not a nerve at fault in them. Not a muscle or tendon laggard.

He glanced back at his watching men. His dark gaze lingered on Vada Conant.

"Rogue, you are hardly in a position to bargain with me. I hold all the advantage."

"Not all, Rico!" Bishop's long fingers shifted ever so slightly, to give point to his demurrer.

Marshal Tom Conant held his breath, blanching at the prospect of a shoot-out, its disastrous consequences. Bishop, he thought, was utterly mad to insert that threat. A recklessly pride-mad gunfighter. Bishop might kill the outlaw *jefe,* but the *guerreros* would cut him down with their ready carbines and afterward they'd make savage work of the captives. They were human wolves, coarsened by long outlawry, consciencelessly brutal.

The marshal didn't realize, or he only dimly realized, in his fright for his daughter, the peculiar nature of the long-standing feud between Bishop and Don Ricardo de Risa. To them it was a personal contest of wits, like a game of chess — chess being a cruelly ruthless war game when played expertly by masters.

The objective was to checkmate the opponent. Defeat him completely. Humble him. Not necessarily to blow his brains out, or his yours, although that became a touch-and-go possibility when strong emotion flared up. Essentially, the game was coolly intellectual.

Bishop and Don Ricardo, having introduced sixguns into it from the first move, and recognizing each other's violent potentials, made their moves with extreme care. One of them *could* get his brains blown out by the other. Right now. To hell with the consequences.

Stalemate, of a sort. Neither player could win until the next move, if then. Irresistible force meeting immovable object.

White queen captured, bishops and knights and rooks nowhere, off the board. Pawns useless. But white king had black king stalemated. With fast-draw guns.

Searching for a temporary compromise to get him off the spot, the don snapped his fingers. "I have it! A bargain!"

"Let's have it," said Bishop skeptically.

"The cattle! Ballinger's steers. I make my offer in generosity to you, old *compadre,* old enemy and friend. Doc has the bill of sale from Ballinger. He will sign it over to you."

Doc Sunday uttered a muffled squawk of protest. The don stared at him pitilessly.

"Treacherous old monkey, you are lucky to be still alive! Here is a pencil. Sign the herd over to Mr. Rogate Bishop — on Ballinger's bill of sale to you, which I'm sure you've got in your pocket!"

Anguishedly, Doc Sunday drew out the paper, unfolded it, scribbled, signed it with his crabbed signature. He passed it to Don Ricardo reluctantly as if giving his life's blood.

Don Ricardo handed it on to Bishop with a grand flourish. "There! A bargain?"

"Those steers," Bishop mentioned, taking the signed document, "are scattered from hell to Christmas, all over this tail-end of Colorado. As for our friend Ballinger, he's in the Trinidad jug for wrecking a train."

"*Que lastima!* We all have our little

troubles."

"Bring out my horse!" Bishop rasped, his temper fraying. He never did have a low boiling-point of temper, particularly when dealing with the don's suave needling.

Don Ricardo smiled at him. His eyes glistened with the glee of a boy stealing apples from the parsonage orchard — for he was and always would be youthful in spirit, a young rebel, to his death. He had once been a swank officer in the Mexican Army, a dashing lieutenant; then general in command of a rabble army of rebels marching against Mexico City's despotism.

The revolution failing, he had become an outlaw chief, the only recourse left to him, fitting to his high-spirited nature and daringly adventurous temperament. Always the chief. No ideals worth the mention. An unprincipled rascal, living day-to-day. His one saving grace was his meticulous courtesy. Spanish punctilio. Relict of a badly tarnished escutcheon.

So he claimed. But he was a deep-dyed liar. Maybe, just maybe, he *had* been an *hidalgo,* a person of importance. He did play with fine verve the part of a dashing caballero. He did have exquisite manners, when called upon.

"It pains me to refuse," he answered in

mock sorrow to Bishop's demand, "knowing how highly you esteem that fine animal. But I must insist on retaining it, at least for a while. It is the only real hold I have on you, to insure myself of your good behavior! That is reasonable, yes?"

"You robber!" Bishop growled at him. "I need a horse! I've got to get back to Trinidad!"

"Why?"

"Ballinger's in jail, I told you. My fault. Got to break him out. D'you know any better reason?"

Don Ricardo shook his head. "No," he replied honestly. One didn't leave a partner in the lurch. That was beyond the pale. You did anything you could for him. "I'll lend you a horse, Rogue. Give you any help I can — but I want your oath first that you won't interfere with Conant's delivery of the money to me! Your sworn oath! I don't trust you, no more than you trust me — but our word of honor still stands good, yes?"

Bishop compressed his wide, hard mouth. The impulse was in him to send the lightning into his prepared hands. He saw that his crimson thought communicated itself to the don, for the don's smile froze instantly. Bishop's glinting eyes roved on, touching

Vada Conant back there captive among the *guerreros.*

He recalled his first impression of Vada. Her lively potentiality of becoming a source of trouble, unwittingly, among raw men. He took no satisfaction in reflecting that he had been right. A lovely young girl was a dreadful responsibility. Big trouble in a small package. A bar to powder-smoke progress.

In a blazing fight she'd be in the way. Get wounded, maybe maimed. No doctor within twenty miles. A man's memory of it would deal him misery the rest of his life.

The don had pulled a neat and simple play, parking the defenseless girl there among his ruffians, in the line of fire. It barred Bishop from making any sudden move to turn the tables on him — always a risk when ace gunfighters got cornered.

"All right, Rico. Agreed. If Conant collects the money from Doc, it's yours, damn you!"

Don Ricardo bowed, clicking his heels in exaggerated officer style, aware that it irritated Bishop. The bright smile on his face was purposely an added exasperation. He was riding the crest of triumph over an old enemy who had too often in the past managed somehow to best him.

"Compromise is the essence of diplomacy!" he stated with fine, fluent sarcasm. "To bargain without anger is a test of mutual faith. Thus we avoid hard feeling between us, yes?"

"Rub it in!" said Bishop. "Have your fun! You promised to lend me a horse, to get me back to Trinidad."

"Yes, but — do you really mean to ride back there? Alone? Openly? That is suicide! I can't believe it!"

"Bring out the horse. You also promised me any help you can give, for *my* promise, didn't you?"

"I did indeed."

"Okay. I'll need a couple of other things for my trip to Trinidad."

"Name them. They are yours." Don Ricardo wagged his head. "*Hombre largo y loco!* Madman . . ."

Trinidad toward the tail-end of the day, sundown, became ordinary and humdrum, for the town was old and settled before the new boom. Housewives called children off the streets for supper, then prayers and bed. Lamps and candles glowed from windows as dusk descended, soon thereafter extinguished.

Visiting cattlemen gather in the eating places. The Mexican end of town wakened from afternoon siesta. In an hour or so more, reversing nature's procedure, Trinidad would bloom alive in the dark dying of day: saloons, gambling houses, dance halls and honky-tonks — all going full blast.

The pattern still held true, despite the eruptions of yesterday. Transient visitors shrugged off that affair. Things happened in a roaring railhead town. The bulk of settled citizens went on about their own business, their first concern being an uninterrupted flow of profit from the boom.

Few cared to ask questions or to show open curiosity in the comings and goings of the Silver Spur mob of marshal's deputies. Queer matters were in the wind. Doc Sunday and Marshal Tom Conant, for instance — driving back into town together in Doc's well-known buckboard, after they both had been seized separately by outlaws and carried off south.

It wasn't wise to press for explanations. Among the townspeople the Silver Spur mob had come to be accepted, vaguely regarded as the marshal's troubleshooters who were trying to keep the town in order. The deputies discouraged questions, with bluntly bullying methods. Very well; keeping peace required the use of force.

The townspeople of Trinidad failed to

draw the line between peace-keeping and outright tyranny. They were paying for their negligence, though so far they were only uneasily conscious of it, of the excesses of crude power in the hands of thugs.

Nobody took more than a fleeting notice of a dozing rider who, in raggedly enveloping poncho and straw sombrero, lazed into town as the sun sank red. A *paisano*. A Mexican peon of no consequence, come to town to spend his few hard-earned dollars on dime-a-glass wine and a gambling fling at monte. Big night for him. In the morning, sick and broke, he'd toil back to his hardscrabble acres, his goats, his adobe shack.

His mount was a ribby grulla nag, the saddle much-mended, the bridle fashioned of greased rope. He drifted across the plaza into the shadow-streaked main street, where he raised his drooping head to look vacantly about him. Languidly, as a tired man of low vitality, he reined his nag to a halt, peering at the painted sign of Doc Sunday's livery stable, and slowly dismounted, dragging his right leg over the shabby saddle as if the effort exhausted him.

For a moment he leaned against his sorry nag, apparently debating with himself whether or not to pay a stabling fee: one dollar per twenty-four hours, grain and hay included; grooming at extra cost. The skinny grulla wouldn't have known ever the touch of brush and comb.

He fished out coins from under his blanket poncho, counted them laboriously, shook his head. No go. Can't afford the dollar — ten glasses of wine. Leave the horse tethered in the street.

Marshal Conant came hurrying out of his office. He gazed about him with the worried look of one who had mislaid and lost something of importance — as he had, for a few lax moments. Not being sharp, Conant had let Doc Sunday get out of his sight, against Don Ricardo's warning. It was a matter perhaps of too much and too long a slavish servitude to power, the power of violence.

He strode over the street to the Silver Spur hitching rack. There, Doc Sunday was examining with professional eye the hoofs of a hind-spotted horse — an appaloosa — or pretending to while conversing rapidly with its owner, who was one of the deputy gun crew. So easy it was to hoodwink the blockhead marshal of Trinidad.

He never should have come in off the open range where he belonged. On the range he was probably a capable man. In town he was out of his natural element.

The rapid conversation broke off as he approached. The owner of the appaloosa horse said briefly, "Okay," and strode into the Silver Spur.

Conant motioned at Doc Sunday to precede him back to his office. Too late. Doc had had time to pass a quickly spoken message. Trying to repair his blunder, Conant stepped close on Doc's heels, darting a stern lookout all around, a shotgun under his right arm. Nothing happened. The scarecrow figure in the ragged poncho was counting his coins over again. The Silver Spur stayed quiet.

Relievedly, Conant steered Doc Sunday off the street and reached the shelter of his office, where he wiped sweat from his forehead, glaring at the little veterinary. He could only hope that his blunder wouldn't ruin Don Ricardo's planned strategy. Maybe Doc hadn't managed to pass a message during those few moments while he was alone with the owner of the spotted horse at the Silver Spur hitchrack.

But if Doc had, if the message was relayed to the deputies — if it cost Don Ricardo de Risa the defeat of his plan and the loss of the forty thousand dollars . . .

"God help us!" Conant breathed. Aloud,

he said to Doc Sunday, "Get the money!"

"It's still too early. I heard de Risa's instructions to you. Not before full sundown do you start for —"

"Get it!" Anxiety thinned Conant's voice. "The money!"

"Not yet. You still have until sundown." Doc Sunday smiled pinchedly. "So have I!"

12

At last the *paisano,* with an air of coming to a weighty decision, led his grulla into the livery stable, where he held up a quarter as a sign that he was solvent and ready to haggle for twenty-five cents' worth of service.

The stableman, lighting lamps and preparing to hitch up a fresh team to Doc Sunday's buckboard, waved him away, too busy to bother with two-bit trade. So he retreated, climbed onto his nag, and drifted off, muttering to himself.

After a while, as all lights came on and the town began stirring, he wandered back again. Lolling dozily in the wornout saddle, straw sombrero tilted low over his bowed face, he nearly got side-swiped by the buckboard and team that wheeled fast out of the livery stable without warning, driven by Marshal Conant. The grulla shied, jolting him upright to hold his seat.

He peered broodingly after the buckboard. He sent an aggrieved look at the livery, and reined over to the town marshal's office. A passing group of cowmen grinned, watching him dismount there and shuffle inside. "Bet he's goin' to make a complaint," one chuckled. "He didn't see it was the marshal hisself. That tarantula juice has sure dimmed his light."

In the marshal's office a deputy, on duty as jailer, ignored the banging of a tin cup on steel bars somewhere in the dark rear. The banging signified that a prisoner was thirsty, but the deputy, lounged in the marshal's chair, wouldn't go to the trouble of taking the man a drink of water. He eyed with intolerant distaste the poncho-draped visitor, who jerked his chin inquiringly toward the sound.

"*Qué hay?*"

"None o' your damn business! If it's the marshal you want, he just left. He won't be back." The deputy took his feet off the desk and clumped them on the floor. "Beat it! You stink!"

"*Pero —*"

"Don't talk that Mex lingo to me!"

"Okay, I won't," said the visitor, and hit him. He hit him with a fist as hard as iron, solidly between the eyes. It lifted the deputy

147

up from the chair and capsized him backward over it. His head struck the wall a fearful crack, like an instant echo of the fist blow. He then lay totally quiet. The banging of the tin cup stopped.

Banjo Ballinger had heard the noise — the deputy's bullying voice, a thud, the crash of the overturned chair and another thud. From his cell, one of two that faced onto a narrow passage, he couldn't see into the marshal's office. He became aware presently of someone or something moving into the passage. Pressing against the bars, he saw a draped figure, a black silhouette, the reflected lamplight from the marshal's office behind it.

It came on, pausing at the door of his cell to peer in at him as if ominously making sure of its victim. A key clinked in the lock. The bolt clicked and the door swung open. Ballinger backed off, fists clenched, vaguely suspecting a lynching bee or a beating. The draped figure didn't inspire trust.

"Don't stand there like a fool!" came the impatient command. "Come on out!"

"You're not the jailer!"

"For once you're right."

"What? Bishop! Lordamighty, I —"

"Pipe down, railroader! Let's not advertise

my presence. It'd give this jail a bad name. Can you make out to ride?"

"Sure. I'm all right." Ballinger's face was bruised and cut. His clothes hung in shreds. But he was young, he'd been bred and raised tough, and he stepped out of the cell like a stallion released. "I was going crazy in there, though," he admitted. "I didn't hardly look for you to break me out."

"I didn't have to break anything except maybe that jailer's head," Bishop mentioned. "Go take his gun. There's a middling good horse over at the saloon rack. A spotted horse. Doc Sunday was prescribing for its feet, but I doubt there's anything wrong with 'em. Get going. I want shed of this poncho. It stinks, like the jailer said. Holds more small game in it than the Apache Reservation."

"Where's Vada? What's happened to her?"

Oh, the single-mindedness of a young man in love. The hot-blooded obsession. The blind idiocy. "Worry about one thing at a time, feller," Bishop counseled. He considered himself superior to such nonsense. He wasn't. "Your first worry is getting a gun and a horse — before somebody comes in to play checkers with the jailer."

Ballinger brushed that aside. A detail of petty importance, entailing merely his life.

"It's Vada I'm —"

"Her father," Bishop interrupted, speaking very distinctly as if to a halfwit, "— her father, Marshal Conant, started out a short while ago in Doc Sunday's buckboard. He's to pay forty thousand dollars to Rico — Don Ricardo de Risa. Ransom for Vada. Got that clear? Now get this. Conant had Doc's old tin box with him in the buckboard. Doc's prescription file. Last place anybody would look for the money, right there in plain sight in the livery stable, day and night. Smart fox, the Doc. I missed out on that. So did Rico."

"Is money all you care about?"

"No, but I don't disrespect it. Now hike on over and lift that horse. I'll cover for you."

Left alone in the marshal's office, absently scratching himself, Bishop concluded he'd had more than enough of the poncho. He had bought it and the straw sombrero from a wood chopper, on his way up from the old Indian mission. The woolen poncho hadn't been washed since it was woven, judging from its ripe fragrance.

It had served him its purpose as far as he cared to use it. He flung it over the senseless jailer-deputy, from whom Ballinger had stripped shell-belt and gun. He drew his squashed black hat from under his coat, punched it back into shape, more or less, and exchanged it for the straw sombrero.

Rummaging shamelessly through Conant's desk, he found a cigar, probably a past gift to the marshal, who didn't smoke cigars. It was crumbly dry. He straightened up from the stoop-shouldered, knee-bent posture that, aided by the poncho, had disguised his height and size.

Feeling more like himself, though itchy in various flea-bitten spots, he chewed on the flaking cigar and gave his attention to the Silver Spur Saloon, a bit tardily. A bartender had emerged, either to view the evening stars, improbably, or for a gulp of fresh air to sustain his lungs through the night in the smoke-filled barroom.

Ballinger was in the process of making acquaintance with the spotted horse, untying its reins, soothing its snuffy disposition with soft-spoken profanity. The animal stamped, snorting, sidling off from his attempt to tighten up the slack cinch. It didn't know him, didn't want to know him.

The bartender cocked his head forward, frowning at the hitchrack. "Hey!" he called. "Get away from that horse! It ain't yours — I know who owns it! Who're you?"

His query brought him an unexpected

reply. Ballinger, exasperated by continued ill-fortune, blasted a shot between his feet. At the same time, Bishop fired over his head, scoring a chance hit on a backbar shelf of bottles inside the Silver Spur. The bartender floundered a backward header through the swingdoors so fast he tore a spring hinge askew, and when the doors flapped closed after him they bonged like a drum.

Bishop jumped out to the grulla, regretting that he hadn't an opportunity to secure a better mount for himself. The grulla wasn't much of a horse. It would have to do. A point in its favor was that it did possess in its scrawny frame the tireless stamina of the wiry mustang breed.

Banjo Ballinger swung onto the spotted horse. Paying no further care to its temperamental fit, he threw his right leg over and clamped it down with a resounding thump that told the snuffy animal who was boss. Cinch still slack, legs gripped to hold the saddle in place, he took off close after Bishop.

"Wish I'd had a bit more time to —"

"You can't have everything your way!"

They rode up the aroused street into the town plaza. Behind them, the damaged swingdoors of the Silver Spur clacked repeatedly, customers spilling out. The plaza, always a favorite haunt of old-timers on warm evenings, was a pool of garrulous reminiscences until the two fleeing riders burst through it, pursued by running townsmen, some of them shooting.

Bishop veered aside from an ancient buffalo hunter who, sniffing battle, possibly an attack by Injun varmints, bemusedly brandished a cap-and-ball pistol as long as his forearm. The big pistol went off and exploded a streak of flame into the air, the old-timer screeching, "Fort in, boys, they's a-comin' at us!"

Bishop struck for the north road out of town. This crazy town of Trinidad where raw crime ran rampant and citizens shot at the wrong folks.

Banjo Ballinger caught up with him on the road, and hurled questions at him. "Where are we going? What happened last night? Did —"

"I told you," Bishop said. "Take your mind off that girl, dammit, and listen! Rico's got her. Conant's on his way to ransom her for forty thousand dollars. Or so he thinks! The gravel pit is the rendezvous. Between here and there, Rico's men are lying in wait to bushwhack the deputies — who Rico expects to chase after Conant. It's not what

I expect."

"Why not?"

"I think Doc Sunday tipped off the deputies. I want to catch Conant before he gets to the gravel pit."

"Bishop, you're not going to stop Conant from delivering the ransom. That's my money, and I'm willing to —"

"It's part mine. I'm not about to let it go for nothing if I can help it."

"Nothing?" Ballinger exclaimed furiously. "Vada's nothing?"

"That's not what I said, blockhead!" Bishop snapped at him. "What's the matter with your horse — or have you forgot how to ride?"

"The saddle's slipping all over."

"Well, pull up and tighten cinch, or you'll rub it raw. I'll push on."

The grulla lumbered rough-gaited, no speed left in it. Bishop relinquished any hope of catching Conant before reaching the gravel pit. The rising moon gave him glimpses of the buckboard far ahead, its fresh team dusting along at a smart pace, but not stretched out. Having cleared town without hindrance, Conant didn't have need to rush. He could lash up a fast run if pressed.

A hint of movement alongside the road

caught Bishop's eye. Rico's men. This was the chosen spot for slaughter. It was a toss-up whether they'd let him pass or shoot him down. He guessed they were trigger-itchy, waiting to ambush the deputies who by Rico's calculations should now be racing in pursuit of Conant and the forty thousand dollars disgorged by Doc Sunday.

Rico was apt to get overconfident, Bishop reflected, whenever he held a winning hand. A flaw in his character.

No sign of the deputies. No pursuit whatever from Trinidad. The would-be ambushers wouldn't wait much longer, feeling frustrated and foolish. Bishop heard a growled mutter of disgust, and the hairs on the back of his neck stopped tingling. Big-hatted figures rose silently and hurried away from the road, to their horses he supposed.

Conant looked rearward, evidently mystified like the *guerreros* at the absence of pursuit. He must have spied Bishop on the road, for he whipped up the team. The buckboard turned off and vanished between two hills.

Reaching the turn-off, Bishop heard the wheels clattering up a stony wagon track into the open gravel pit. He took the unlighted cigar from his mouth, half minded to send a hail after Conant to turn back,

155

then shook his head. No good. The marshal wasn't in the least likely to obey any such summons from him.

Banjo Ballinger came pounding up behind. "De Risa's men are coming," he announced. "What'll we do?"

"We don't make any sudden moves," Bishop said, "or they're liable to take out their disappointment on us."

"Disappointment?"

"They figured on wiping out the Silver Spur mob. One of Rico's little surprises. But it fizzled. So they're not in a happy humor, you can bet. Let's mosey on. Too late to turn back now, anyway — those carbines are set to pop off at anything moving."

The gravel pit was a huge hole gouged out of the sloping bowl between the hills, with the wagon track its only feasible entrance or exit. With so much of the hillsides cut away, what was left formed a high, circular cliff around the broad pit. Cutting had been done on the wagon road, too, to grade it for the work mules. Following it into the gravel pit was somewhat like riding along a wide vestibule into a roofless arena.

Walking the grulla, Bishop came out onto the floor of the excavation. He ranged a sharp look about him, checking all points, distrustful of the place although it appeared to be empty except for Conant, who had halted his team. Banjo Ballinger looked searchingly about, too, but he was looking only for Vada.

Conant got down from the buckboard, staring back at the two horsemen. The high banks shut out the low moon, keeping the gravel pit sunk in deep shadow. A broken-down gravel wagon stood abandoned, rocks and rubbish thrown on and around it. Prudently, Conant, shotgun raised, edged toward the rubbish heap for cover.

"Hold it!" Bishop said.

"Oh, it's you, Bishop." Conant didn't sound very reassured. As a courier bearing ransom, he knew that his position was hazardous on all sides. The stolen money was a magnet to ruthless men — Don Ricardo de Risa, Bishop, Doc Sunday and the Silver Spur mob of deputies. Killers all.

Bishop listened to oncoming riders. He heard them leave the road and turn onto the wagon track. Exit blocked. He again cast a look around, but noted only that the foreman's shack still remained. The shack was built atop the highest bank, to enable the foreman to oversee the digging below and spot any pick-and-shovel stiff loafing on the job. Moonlight touched the upper part of it, giving it a ghostly illusion of suspending in space. It was too far up to get to in a hurry. He prepared to face Don Ricardo and his unmerry men, while meantime wondering about the deputies.

13

"Hello, Rogue!"

Don Ricardo stepped from behind the rubbish heap, with Vada before him. He held a gun cocked and leveled in his right hand, and his eyes glinted wickedly.

"So you broke your word and tried for the money! That costs you your good black horse. Possibly more. Certainly more if you dare make a move!"

He meant it. He could play a cutthroat game with flowery punctilio and finesse, enjoying it, but in the actual payoff he was altogether a different kind of man.

Caught napping, Bishop hid his chagrined surprise. He had supposed that the don was with his men or somewhere near by. Tardily, he remembered that it was usually a mistake to rest on supposition when it involved Don Ricardo.

"I came after Conant," he said, "because I thought the deputies might have got here

first. I can't figure where else they'd be."
He wasn't accustomed to speaking in de-
fense of his actions; it increased his chagrin.
"Don't take that tone to me, damn you!"

The riders trooped in off the wagon track,
ominously somber, touchy as tigers after
their failure to ambush the detested gringo
deputies. Seeking scapegoats to blame for
the fiasco, they glowered menacingly at
Bishop and Ballinger, at Conant, at the girl.
Gringos . . .

"Conant, warn your daughter to keep
still!" rapped the don crisply. "And you,
Ballinger, stay where you are! Our business
is not yet finished. Where is the money, Conant?"

"In a box in the buckboard. Doc's prescription box."

"What? His — ? I never thought of that! I
told you to tie the money in a sack to your
saddle."

"There wasn't time, and I couldn't handle
the box on a horse. Doc wouldn't give up
the money till the last minute. The buckboard was ready, so I took it. That's all."

Don Ricardo frowned. Things weren't
running tidily according to plan. Strange,
that the deputies hadn't come streaming
after Conant. Doc Sunday, forced to relin-
quish the forty thousand dollars, should

naturally have raised an alarm as soon as Conant made his dash with it out of Trinidad.

Something had gone amiss. "Did you allow Doc Sunday out of your sight?" he demanded of Conant. "Did he get any chance to warn the deputies beforehand?"

"No," Conant lied, fearful of confessing his blunder.

"What happened in town while you waited for sunset?"

"Nothing that I could see. I kept him close by me in my office. The deputies didn't show themselves at all."

"That seems odd," the don murmured. "Where were they, I wonder? Well, the money . . ." He stepped toward the buckboard.

Bishop narrowed further attention up at the foreman's shack. The light from the rising moon, inching down it, showed it in full. Gravel had been dug away so deeply from beneath its floor that it protruded halfway out over the edge of the steep bank, which was what helped to create the illusion that the shack hung suspended in space.

Those pick-and-shovel stiffs had evidently exercised their Irish sense of humor, slyly digging away the foundation as a practical joke on their boss. But the boss had caught

161

on and made them brace up the floor with timber stilts, dashing their sinful hopes of seeing him and his establishment capsize down the bank. There it perched, sturdily constructed of rejected railroad ties, much like a shotgun tower overlooking a prison yard — which was probably how the Irish laborers had viewed it, wishful to throw rocks at the boss's face watching them relentlessly from its glassless window. Stop for a smoke, and the bull voice of him blared down at you. Bejayzus, in the Ould Country he'd get short shrift.

No boss was up there now. He and the gravelers and graders had gone on south with the extending roadbed, far on ahead of the rails. But there was movement within the glassless window, a silent gathering of faces in the dark interior and dull flickers of metal.

Don Ricardo, starting to reach into the buckboard for the box, turned a brittle stare on Bishop. "Don't shift, Rogue! You'll die, I swear, if you try to pull —"

"To hell with that!" Bishop grunted, sliding fast off the grulla and crouching low. *"Look up at the shack!"*

The don refused to take his eyes off Bishop. He wasn't to be thrown off-guard by a stale ruse. Seeing Bishop's pair of heavy guns streak up, he dodged nimbly and rapped, "Hombres! Shoot the mad gringo!"

A volley of gunfire thundered, deafening in the enclosed hollow of the gravel pit. Not from the carbines. From the shack above, where shooters crowding the long, gaping window blazed rapid-fire down at the group.

Chips of stone flew in the whistling drone of ricochet bullets. The shooters, moonlight in their eyes on their height, poured shots at every murky shadow below, indiscriminately, relying on volume. Banjo Ballinger's spotted horse, fairly conspicuous in any kind of light, dropped as if slammed by a sledgehammer. Two *guerreros* let their carbines fall and clutched at each other for support, one wagging his head as if to deny a brutal fact. A horse tore squealing around the pit, driving the rest wild.

Bishop punched the grulla, got it headed toward the broken wagon and rubbish heap, and ran alongside it for cover, Banjo Ballinger close behind him. They passed the buckboard, its rearing team swinging it this way and that, and Don Ricardo raced around it to join them in their dash. The panicked grulla swerved off-course, and Bishop and the don sprinted the rest of the way without it. Quick on his feet, the don

163

got first to the rubbish heap and burrowed under the broken wagon. Bishop dived in on top of him. Banjo had gone off at a tangent with the grulla, apparently losing his sense of direction in the chaos.

Don Ricardo said things muffledly in two languages, his wind squashed out by Bishop's dive onto him. He squirmed free of the crushing weight, sat up, and cracked his head against the bottom of the wagon. His bilingual swearing reached lurid perfection. Bishop poked him in the eye with an ungentle elbow.

"Quit singing misery! It's bad enough as 'tis."

The don wiped his eye, swearing some more. "Where are those shots coming from?"

"The shack. Dammit, I told you to look up!"

"How do I know when to believe you!"

Three of the don's men made a break for the wagon track, one riding, the other two hanging on. The gravel pit was rapidly becoming a shambles. Shots lashed at the three. The sharpshooters above had that exit covered. The rider spilled with his horse, and the two runners huddled flat. No escape by that route.

Bishop's dark, strong face grew saturnine.

This was slaughter, an intended massacre, like shooting fish in a barrel. And he was one of the fish. The broken wagon and rubbish heap could only provide temporary cover for a last stand.

"It's the Silver Spur mob," he said to Don Ricardo. "The deputies. Doc Sunday tipped the word to them in Trinidad before sundown, when Conant wasn't watching him. They slipped out of town and rounded here ahead of us. So much for your bright idea of ambushing 'em!"

"The boot is on the other foot," admitted the don sourly. "They ambushed *us!*"

"Yeah. And the law's on their side. They'll lay out our dead carcasses for public display in the Trinidad plaza. Victory for law and order. A warning example. Poor end for us, Rico! Do we take it?"

"Never!"

Vada Conant had caught the flying reins of a loose horse, but it stopped a bullet or two while she strove to mount onto the Mexican high-cantled saddle. The horse skittered half around and fell on her, pinning her leg under it, foot in the tapadera stirrup. Banjo Ballinger ran to help her. Nothing was wrong with his sense of direction where she was concerned. He strained to heave the dead horse off her leg. A dead horse is a dead weight, more than most men can shift, and Banjo's efforts failed. Bullets flailing the ground, he scrunched beside Vada, both using the dead horse for meager shelter while he kept on working to free her. Tom Conant ran stumbling to help.

Bishop backed out from under the wagon. "Come on, then!" he rasped at Don Ricardo. "Ballinger's trying to bring in the girl. He can't do it. Let's give him a hand, caballero!"

"*Ay di mi!* Must we?"

"He's one of us. And there's the girl."

"Ah, yes, the girl . . ."

Often, in expansive mood, Don Ricardo de Risa claimed to be a descendant of high-born lineage, noble Spanish blood. A black-sheep descendant, obviously. When drunk, he elevated to royal blueblood and was liable to become imperially courtly.

At that, Bishop sometimes almost believed a tenth of the grandiose claims, for the don was occasionally capable of exalted gallantry that surprised even himself. He was at his best in disaster, as long as he could meet disaster with a flourish. And he could still polish up a tarnished chivalry toward women, pretty women, preferably young and tender.

He crawled from under the wagon, bone-handled guns cocked, and nearly got buried under five of his men plunging to the cover of the rubbish heap.

"Up! Up, I say! Follow me, *mis valientes!*"

It might have been the compliment he paid them — calling them valiant, which at present they definitely weren't. Or his crackling tone of command. He had a talent for rallying defeated men, certainly. By power of will, and by his electric personality, he made them believe in him. His gaudy swank passed for superb confidence. They followed him and Bishop in a rush to the fallen horse, firing upward on the run.

The outburst, like a diehard charge of doomed men, caused a moment's astonished break in the shooting from the shack. They rolled the dead horse over while Bishop and Don Ricardo blazed at the window. Banjo Ballinger lifted up Vada. He bumped into Tom Conant attempting the same thing. They both rushed her off between them. Gunfire blared anew from the shack.

"Back, *mis valientes! Pronto!*"

The retreat cost two men slain. Tall price for the life of a *gringa* girl, in the hard estimation of *hombres del campo.* Only money was worth fighting for. *Dinero.* For lavish squandering. A woman could be abducted easily, often willingly, from drudgery in a sunbaked village.

The mound of quarry rubbish made a fairly good shield from the shack marksmen, but it was cramped quarters. Three more of the don's men, two wounded, crawled in desperately seeking shelter, crowding the limited capacity. They and the others snapped off carbine shots at the shack.

"Aim at the window," Bishop said. "Not the walls. Too thick. Railroad ties."

He rummaged into the rubbish heap. The shack was utterly impregnable to bullets. The deputies in it, forsaking its gaping window, fired out through the uncaulked chinks between the railroad ties. Hitting a chink at this distance and angle, in moonlight was a slim chance. A different means had to be found to combat the deputies.

"What the devil are you searching for?" inquired the don.

"Something like this," Bishop answered. He dragged forth a wornout crowbar from the rubble. "It might do."

The crowbar was split at one end, mushroomed at the other, worthless. It was long and heavy, what railroad graders called a pinch bar, used for prying rails, for any job requiring mighty leverage, generally by a pair of big-muscled workers, a third man striking its blunt head with a sledgehammer to gain deeper purchase when needed. Grasping it, getting the feel of its weight, Bishop surveyed the distance to the foot of the cut-away bank below the shack. An open expanse, not yet touched by moonlight; but it was visible to the deputies. He wished the moon didn't rise so fast — it wasn't giving him much time to make up his mind.

"Rico," he said, "tell your hombres to fire everything they've got loaded. I want 'em to cover for me. For a minute, that's all."

"Where are you going?"

"To the shack, if I can get there. Want to come along?"

"You madman!" muttered Don Ricardo. "It is — what is the word? Impregnable!" With a rare tinge of friendship, a holdover from other days of fighting side-by-side, he said, "*Compadre* — don't throw your life away!"

"What's it worth here in a trash pile? And yours? All of us. Follow me, *valiente!*" Bishop mocked him. Lugging the wornout pinch bar, he sprang up and started his long-legged sprint across the open bed of the gravel pit.

A bullet from the shack whipped stones

before him. Too hurried, that shooter, too low, result of bad light and overeager trigger. Another bullet clanged off the pinch bar. The shock of it stung his gripping fingers. He thought the don's remaining men behind the rubbish heap would never fire, that they must have abandoned him, let him go alone in a suicidal assault. Mad gringo.

Then suddenly they fired. It was a crashing volley of carbines and sixguns, aimed mainly at the shack window and splintering its rough frame. Rico had made them come through, by cajolery and threats. Good man in a pinch, Rico, despite many grave faults.

Racing to the shack in the uproar, Bishop hoped its floorboards were tightly fitted, that by getting underneath the protruding section of floor he'd be out of the line of fire and unhindered in his purpose. His hope dissipated as soon as he reached the foot of the cutbank and began climbing up it. A shot speared at him from between dry-shrunk and warped floorboards. The deputies had him spotted.

He drew one gun, took aim, and spaced three shots at the spot. Somebody up in the shack wailed and fell. There were scrabbling sounds of the hit man being pulled aside.

Bishop went on climbing. It was awkward,

the heavy steel pinch bar dragging from one hand, gun in the other, the gravel bank steep and loose to the footing.

Rapid reports stabbed from the same spot in the floor, then from another. He sighted a shot upward, and two more spots spurted alive. They were onto him. Never mind the rubbish heap for now. Get the big fellow, the one-man charging brigade, before he did damage. Bishop swore, doubting if he could make it up alive and alone. He'd be in moonlight up there, a stark target for them at point-blank range, allowing that he got that far.

Yet he couldn't stay where he was, part way up the bank. Couldn't foretell where, in the overhanging floor, the next shots would come from. The deputies only had to poke guns through gaps in the thick, un-planed boards, while he had to wait for a flash to shoot at, the floor being in shadow. It came to him that he had maneuvered himself into a bind.

A deafening discharge roared behind his back, and he slung violently around, glaring, ears ringing.

14

Smoke of black powder wisping from the muzzle of a thumb-size caliber carbine, Don Ricardo agilely ducked the sweep of the pinch bar.

"Phew! You're sharp on the prod, Rogue! I'm here to cover for you, you madman. What's that iron bar for? What are you trying to do?"

Bishop paid him a ghost of a grin.

Good man, Rico, yes. Tricky scoundrel. Double-crossing thief. Bandit, soldier of fortune, renegade for profit. But a damned good man to have along in a bad bind.

"I'm trying to get up under the shack. To bust it down. I need your help."

"That you do!"

A glitter brightened the don's dark eyes. The wicked mischief of Bishop's intention appealed to him strongly. At a time like this he and the big gringo gunfighter were *compadres,* brothers-in-arms, grudges laid aside, their feud temporarily shelved.

"Onward and upward, *valiente!*"

Bishop climbed the bank, no longer troubling to watch for flashes from between the floorboards above him. Rico was on ready watch. Rico had cat-eyes, could see in the dark, and he was a fast shot — possibly the fastest and most deadly accurate shot ever to come north out of Chihuahua.

A head poked from a side window of the shack. A rifle slid swiftly forth, canting downward at the two climbing figures below. Don Ricardo fired at a crack between floorboards, shifted aim, and fired again, a shaved fraction of a second between his shots. The rifle tumbled out of the window, landing on the steep slope where it rolled on down. Its owner's head and forearms sank onto the sill and draggingly withdrew from sight.

"Pretty good shooting, Rico," Bishop said. He couldn't have done better. "Maybe you're not slowing off, after all."

"Me slowing? I'm still the best —"

"Quit bragging and watch the floor!"

Clawing to the foot of a corner post, Bishop hauled himself upright and, with some difficulty, obtained footing by stamping his boot heels into the shale. He studied briefly the log supports of the shack, their arrangement, seeking a possible key to weakness. Examined close-up, the logs were much more sturdy than they had appeared to be at a distance. They were well placed and bedded. That pick-and-shovel boss should have been a construction engineer; he had set the props in right.

Selecting one at random, Bishop dug and pried at its foot. It resisted his efforts. Exasperated, he swung the heavy pinch bar and with all his strength hit the prop a mightly wallop that dislodged it and sent a shudder up to the shack. That, then, was the solution. Brute force. He went to work on another prop, slamming it askew.

Don Ricardo chuckled, spacing shots up at the over-hanging floor. "Brawny Samson! Go on — crack the pillars of the temple of sin! The damned Philistines are worrying like rats in a sinking ship! Hear them?" He once had captained a stolen schooner, gun runner, semi-pirate, until South American gunboats shelled him out of that phase in his lurid career.

The men inside the shack were shouting at one another, arguing. Their voices could be plainly heard through the riven floor. Shang Tate proposed a swarm-out, a fast shooting down at the impertinently prickly pair below. That was Shang Tate's bombastic style. He hadn't learned his lesson. Green gunman, full of fire and slaughter, carrying a hot grudge.

Somebody else offered a different suggestion. "Rip out a plank in the floor an' blast hell at 'em! Them two are fast sharpshots, Shang!"

"I ain't no slouch, neither, comes to a gun!"

"D'you want to go first out the door? Go ahead! Not me! Rogue Bishop — de Risa . . . Gunfighting's their life-long trade. Rip up a plank, stay to cover here, an' blast 'em dead!"

The idea drew approval from others of the Silver Spur mob, one of them rasping urgently, "Goddam it, let's get to it before they capsize this cussed shebang! I can feel the floor kinda sink. Quick, or get out!"

They didn't have tools. They used rifle barrels to lever loose a plank, its extracted nails groaning. The plank, straight-grained, split with a dry crack in its middle. Cursing it, they shoved the broken length of timber aside and pried at the remaining half.

Don Ricardo looked thoughtful then, as if seriously contemplating a quick retreat. He was a chill realist behind all his gaudy flair, sensibly rejecting the profitless merit of staying with a lost cause to its bitter end. By that rule of philosophy, ironly self-centered, he had so far survived. The Trinidad deputies up in the shack, once they gapped the floor, would be able to blaze down blind from cover.

"Stick, Rico!" Bishop called to him. "Cover for me just a minute more, *amigo!*"

Amigo. Not for a long time had Don Ricardo de Risa heard the big gringo call him that.

Amigo — friend. More than mere friend, in the old sense prevailing among men of the gunfighting brotherhood, a breed not given to using the term loosely. To them, at least, *amigo* still meant a true side-kick, steadfast — though it could be only temporary, future circumstances setting them on opposite sides. The new crop of gunsters, now prevalent, had defaced the coin of the term until it had no value among their kind.

Bishop struck mightily again, knocking out another prop. The don looked even more pensively thoughtful when the shack lurched over unevenly a few inches. He and Bishop were directly beneath the sagging floor. It sagged further, timbers creaking and grinding together, after the next smite of the pinch bar.

Streaming sweat, his muscles aching from the immense efforts he had imposed on himself, and his hands almost numb, Bishop grunted, "Out, Rico — next'll do it! Guard the door!"

"You — ?"

"Goddam it, do as I say!"

Don Ricardo backed out from under the buckling floor of the shack, thankfully, having a horror of being buried alive. The broken rim of the shale bank was cascading down. He scrambled up the bank. The door of the shack scraped open a foot, then stuck, its frame twisted out of kilter. Men inside shoved and kicked at it, trying to squeeze through. The don's guns, blaring, drove them back, lacking one who hung pinched in the opening, filling it, groaning faintly.

Bishop smashed out the last prop, a corner post that held the shack leaning askew. He dropped the pinch bar, sprang clear, and flattened out on the gravel, spreading his aching arms wide to keep himself from rolling down.

The shack teetered on the bank's high rim. The men inside it might, if they had kept their heads, have crowded to the rear and used their combined weight to hold it in balance. They didn't. Disorganized, they were all shouting at cross-purposes, the tilting floor sliding them forward and adding their weight to the overbalance of the shack.

It keeled over, slowly and ponderously, then with gathering momentum, law of gravity. Its floor gouged the rim, breaking loose showers of gravel. It tipped abruptly, nosing downward. A figure spilled from the up-ended rear door, taking a flying leap, and Don Ricardo whipped a shot at it while it was still in the air and brought it down spraddled like a hit duck.

The shack capsized end-over-end twice down the steep bank, logs and boards bursting from it, shedding roof shingles. It crashed wrecked at the bottom. Damaged men inside it could be heard mumbling dazedly after it slumped to rest, half buried in the slide of gravel.

"Shook 'em up like dice in a cup," Bishop commented satisfiedly, working the numbness from his hands and stretching his aching shoulder muscles. The wound in his thigh smarted. His exertions had broken the clotted blood, causing the wound to bleed afresh. Tomorrow he'd be stiff and sore, needing to take care of himself somehow, somewhere.

"Shook them down," corrected Don Ricardo, a stickler for precision in language. "Ah, that was fun, Rogue!" he exulted. "Magnificent stroke — snatching victory from the jaws of defeat! Reminds me of —"

"Never mind the memories. Listen! D'you hear what I hear?"

After the final crash of the shack and the settling of fallen gravel, another sound intruded: a distant drumming of hoofs on hard earth.

Their eyes met, knowledgeably alert, the don nodding slightly. "I hear it. A posse, coming up from Trinidad, eh? A large posse. All citizens willing and able. Ranch horses —"

"Let's ki-yi out o' here! We've got what we came for. It's in the buckboard."

"Bueno!"

Sliding down the bank with Bishop, the don called to the remainder of his men, "To your horses, quick!" in *pocho* Spanish, border Mexican. "Guard the buckboard — it contains money for us!"

The hard-bitten *guerreros* darted to the scattered horses. Despite their air of lazy shambling, they had fleetness of foot when emergency demanded it. They sped with a kind of shuffling agility, each capturing a horse, earing it down, mastering it, then providently testing the snorting animal's cinch before mounting.

Bishop singled out his big black horse in the ruckus, and made for it. He had never taught the black any tricks, such as coming to his whistle, nor even given it a name except, "Hi, you."

A horse was merely a means of travel, of getting from one place to another. No sentiment involved. If the horse was a good one, you took care of it. Scrupulous care. It fed and watered first, saddle off and a rubdown, before you took your ease. Bishop subscribed to that.

"Hi, you!" he said to the black.

The big horse stopped, stock-still, showing the whites of its eyes, ears laid back. Like its master, it disliked any touch of sentiment. A stroking hand on its neck, particularly on its nuzzle, could receive a wicked bite. A mean-natured brute, that only Bishop could handle.

"Hold it, you!" Bishop growled. "Bite at me, I'll knock your head off!" He swung up into the saddle, clamping his long legs down. "We go, you!"

That was language the horse appreciated, sensing and sharing the man's satisfaction at their reunion. It was attached to Bishop, as Bishop was to it — more like partners than man and animal, for they had weathered together much turbulence in the past. They trusted each other.

The big black paced forward under rein, head high, holding itself haughtily aloof from the rush of common horses, while at the same time managing to jostle to the front easily, bumping off competitors. It stood nearly eighteen hands high. A lot of horse, for a lot of rider. Bishop was six-three and weighed close to two hundred, no fat.

They swarmed through the wagon track out onto the road. Southward, they could see in the distance, the moon rising, a dark bulge moving fast up from the direction of Trinidad: horsemen, a citizens' posse. Trinidad was up in arms, sternly bent upon eradicating the outlaws who had played havoc with their fair city. Outlaws who, furthermore, were rumored to have extracted a fortune in cash from Doc Sunday. Cash . . .

"Head north to the old Delagua trail!" Don Ricardo ordered Banjo Ballinger, who drove the buckboard. Tom Conant and his daughter rode in it, Conant squeezing a bullet-torn and bloody shoulder, Vada lamed by her wrenched ankle. "Turn west at the cut-off!"

"What hide-out are you making for, Rico?" Bishop inquired. He felt sure that the don didn't possess extensive knowledge of this south Colorado country, only a general idea of it.

"Then we swing back south, to hit the

Taos road again below Trinidad!" the don commanded.

He rode alongside the buckboard, personally guarding his prize in it, Doc Sunday's tin prescription box. To Bishop's query, he answered tardily, offhand, "No hide-out. It's back to Mexico for me, *muy pronto,* with my hard-earned profits! You will soon leave us, eh?"

"I reckon so. And Conant and Ballinger. *And* the girl!"

"They're hostages! In case pursuit —"

"Sure. That's understood. I'll ride along till you feel safe to turn your hostages loose, unharmed. Okay?"

Don Ricardo's response to that was an eloquent shrug of his shoulders, meaning, "If you must cross me, so be it!" The truce between him and Bishop was already wearing thin. They were too proudly individualistic to get along together for more than the space of an extreme emergency. And too resolutely at loggerheads over the deadly serious matter of loot.

"I could spare Conant and Ballinger, I suppose," he offered tentatively in bargain.

"Don't get bighearted," Bishop returned drily. The don hadn't any need for hostages now. He and his few remaining *guerreros* could take to the roughs, if pressed, and lose the pursuing Trinidad posse in the dark. Conant and Ballinger were more of an encumbrance to him than an asset. He was willing to be rid of them. Empty deal.

Presently, before reaching the old Delagua cut-off, Bishop began having trouble from the *guerreros.* Riding like the superb horsemen that they were, they persistently tried to maneuver themselves into closing in behind and around him. Their *jefe* had got a signal to them.

He abruptly veered off aside, keeping sharp watch on them; whereupon they, knowing he had caught on, gazed ahead impassively as if he didn't exist. As if they weren't keenly aware of the lightning capacity of his guns. The buckboard careened past a curve, Bishop riding apart, Don Ricardo close by it, possessively.

The game of trickery was on again. End of truce. Once more, Bishop found himself holding scrap cards against the aces of his wily old enemy, winner take all, loser to hell. Don Ricardo, damn him, had this game sewed up tight. He had the winnings in his grasp — plunder and a pretty girl. He could afford to offer a cynical deal, one that rid him of inconvenient encumbrances in his dash back home to Mexico.

"I'm sticking along, Rico!" Bishop called

to him, heavily, in an attempt to crack the don's cocksureness.

No go. "Nice to have you, Rogue!" the don replied with mocking courtesy. "But it is a long way down to the border. A good three hundred miles. Five days ride or more. What will you do for sleep?"

"Same as you. One eye open."

"Food, drink?"

"I'll make out."

"*Hombre largo y loco!* What can make you quit?"

"Try killing me. Just try, you bastard!"

"Not now. Not this night. Later . . ."

15

They soon left the old Delagua trail. It had originally crossed the river, but the ford, silting up, made for a chancy crossing. They struck south, more or less following the bank of the river, a rider scouting forward to pick the most feasible route for the buckboard.

The lights of Trinidad came up on their left. Avoiding them, the party cut onto the Taos road well below town. The road was empty. They were on the loose, free of pursuit. The *guerreros* slid carbines into saddle boots, rolled brown cigarettes and lighted up. Barring unforeseen obstacles, they were homeward bound — with money, gringo cash. Don Ricardo de Risa had a fine reputation for sharing generously with his followers. Caballero. Too few left like him these days. He had his faults, *si,* but they were gallant faults in the ancient conquistador tradition. To ride with him was a privilege requiring a disregard for death, including one's own. He himself bore a charmed life, doubtless by satanic favor.

Banjo Ballinger suddenly pulled the team to a halt, causing the riders to halt behind. Don Ricardo frowningly demanded to know the reason; he evidently suspected some kind of collusion between Bishop and Ballinger, a trick, for he swiftly palmed a gun butt.

"There's a saddled horse tied in the brush," Banjo said, pointing off the road. Being foolish about horses, he couldn't bring himself to pass by one that might be abandoned, suffering from thirst and hunger.

The don, who was also a lover of horses — he stole them at every opportunity — snapped to one of his men, "Go get it, Chapalillo! Look around for what else may be there, *pronto.*"

Chapalillo, a battle-scarred little Yaqui half-breed, reined his horse off the road and went smashing through the thick brush. He was a ready scrapper endowed with alert Indian instincts, a valuable man. How he had come by his curious name was anybody's guess.

"Only the horse, *mi jefe,*" he called after circling through the brush around it. "A fine *moreno* horse! Oh, fine!"

"Bring it out."

"Is mine?"

"Is yours."

"*Gracias,*" said Chapalillo. "Is —" He broke off, exclaiming a muttered, *"Mil diablos!"*

He had stumbled upon someone crouched hiding in the brush: the skulking owner of that fine *moreno* horse. His blurt to a thousand devils — *mil diablos* — brought him no aid. The discharge of a pistol stopped his voice. A .44 derringer, from the sound of it, snub-barreled, most likely a two-shot pocket pistol of the type worn in hidden under-sleeve harness by the professional gamblers and their ilk. On the shot of the pistol, the tethered horse reared, breaking loose. It trotted out onto the road, snorting. Chapalillo followed more slowly, clasping his left side.

"*El veterinario . . .*" he mumbled, and fell from his saddle.

"Doc Sunday," said Conant, nodding. "That horse there belongs to him. From his ranch. Got his brand on it." He climbed down from the buckboard. Bracing himself with visible effort, he walked off the road.

"Come back here!" Don Ricardo called after him.

Ignoring the command, Conant plodded on into the brush. A moving body rustled furtively ahead of him. He could be heard to stalk it steadily, making no attempt at quietness. Presently the sounds ceased, stalker and stalked both at a standstill somewhere among the bushes.

The thin, high voice of Doc Sunday piped, "I've got you, Conant! You fool — !"

Brush crackled, evidently from Conant's instant dive. His gun rapped across the report of the derringer, then discharged two more shells after a short pause.

Conant reappeared, walking slowly. Reaching the road, he halted to stare about him as if surprised to find himself there. "I've taken my last order from him," he announced to nobody in particular. "He's dead — real dead! I killed him!"

"Congratulations!" said Don Ricardo sardonically. "But why was he there? What was he trying to do, alone there in the chaparral at night?"

"I got no idea. He never did it before, to my knowledge."

"Strange! He couldn't have known we would come this way. Even if he had, he wouldn't have waited alone with only a pocket pistol. He would have set up an ambush, to get back the money in that tin box." The don shook his head. "I have a feeling that something is wrong! Open the box for me."

"I don't have the key to it," Conant answered him. "The money's there, though. Doc showed me. But he wouldn't give me the key. He never trusted a livin' soul where cash is concerned."

"Neither do I!" The don took the tin box from the buckboard. He drew a gun and put its muzzle to the lock, frowning. "It weighs light!"

Bishop guessed it would. Estimating the near-future prospects, he foresaw explosions, himself in the midst with only his wits to ward off disaster. The *guerreros*, drawn carbines resting across their saddles, hungrily waited to see money in bills of large denomination, while keeping watch on him. Conant and Banjo were on the spot, too. In the buckboard, Vada sat disabled from running.

A shot mangled the lock. The lid of the box was flung open. For a moment there was stunned silence.

Don Ricardo de Risa began muttering in a strangled whisper. Rage reddened his face. His muttering rose, the phrases becoming coherent, all of them sizzlingly profane except the final word — "Empty!"

"So it is," Bishop confirmed. "Not a dollar in it." He swept a quick glance over the *guerreros.* Their mood had abruptly changed from bright expectation to furious dismay. They snapped up their carbines, craving to kill someone as an expression of their feelings.

"Empty!" the don repeated in a snarl, hurling down the tin box and kicking it. He spun around and glared at Conant. "You! The money, you said, was in the box! You lied to me!"

Conant shook his head confusedly. "I saw it there, I swear! I had Doc Sunday unlock the box and show me, not long before I started out with it to the gravel pit."

"Then where is it, damn you?" Like his men, the don sought a scapegoat or two. Or three. He whipped out both of his guns.

"Use some sense, Rico," Bishop advised.

The don turned on him, glittering-eyed. "Rogue Bishop, don't you cross me now!" He was as taut as a drawn bowstring. The blood rushed from his face, leaving it deadly pale, giving it a look of sudden thinness. The carbines clicked, cocked, leveled ready.

"You'll be crossing yourself if you cut loose!"

"I'll take that chance!"

Bishop shrugged, feigning an easiness that he didn't feel. He and Don Ricardo had never been closer to a point-blank, face-to-face showdown, and this time all the odds lay on the don's side. "I mean Ballinger's forty thousand dollars. You'd never get your hands on it again, whichever way the smoke blew."

"I can force Conant to tell me where —"

"He can't, because he doesn't know. You're blaming him for taking the money, but I wager he never had it in the first place. He only thought he did."

"You're trying one of your tricks!" the don snapped. "A bluff!"

"No, this is on the level. Conant drove the buckboard, and he didn't stop anywhere till he got to the gravel pit. He left town fast. You were covering part of the road, and I was behind him the rest of the way. He couldn't have got at the box. Nobody's had a chance to touch it till now. Yet it's empty. What's the answer?"

"I am not in the humor for puzzles!"

"Conant," Bishop asked the marshal, "who lifted the box into the buckboard in the livery, you or Doc Sunday?"

"He did. But, look, he'd showed me previously —"

"Sure. He let you glimpse some money

he'd put in it, to satisfy you. Not Ballinger's forty thousand dollars, though. I figure he'd already put that out of reach. Then," Bishop went on, "when maybe you weren't watching him, Doc pulled a switch on you. A shell-game switch. Now you see it, now you don't!"

Conant knuckled his forehead. "I never learn! Doc must have sneaked the money out quick while I was locking up my office."

Bishop nodded. "If anything had been in the box when you drove out of the livery, it would still be there. Stands to reason. You satisfied, Rico?"

"No! It seems evident that Doc Sunday hoodwinked Conant — but satisfied I am not! That slippery old *zorro!*" the don grated. "Forty thousand dollars, hidden only he knew where! Even by his death he cheats me of it! Are you sure you killed him, Conant?"

"I shot him through the heart, if he had one!"

"*Mil maldiciónes!* What a blundering fool you are! I could have wrung the secret out of him, alive! You have cost me —"

"Quit the funeral dirge," Bishop interposed. "Conant didn't know then about the box being empty. None of us knew, till you broke it open. It's just bad luck all round."

192

"*He* is the bad luck!" spat Don Ricardo. "You had better take him out of my sight before I shoot him! We part company here. Leave the buckboard, Ballinger!" He held his guns trained directly at Bishop. The cocked carbines covered Banjo Ballinger and Conant, eyes above them wickedly impatient, bearing the message: Death to the gringos at the slightest excuse. Give us the excuse, gringos! *Por favor!*

Banjo Ballinger, holding onto the lines of the team, dared to raise an objection. "We'll need this buckboard," he said, "for Vada. She's got a wrenched ankle."

"I know she has."

"Then if you've got any human feeling —"

"Oh, I have — I have!" the don interrupted. He smiled, reverting to his normal suave self. His handsome, slightly blunted features smoothed, the angry disappointment ironed out. "My human feeling demands that the lovely young lady must travel in comfort. That," he said blandly, "is why *I* shall need the buckboard!"

He was once more the debonair Laughing One, the mocking caricature of a grand caballero, with exaggerated punctilio and tarnished honor. Only bad temper coarsened him, and it never lasted. His dangerousness lasted always, whatever his mood.

To make his meaning perfectly clear, he added with elegant delicacy, "The fresh bloom of her health must be conserved. I do not wish her to become overly fatigued by the journey to Mexico. Her ankle will mend on the way, given care. Vacate the buckboard, Ballinger!"

Banjo's whole body gave a convulsive jerk as if a dagger pricked him. He glared hollow-eyed at the don, while his lips worked soundlessly. Anguishedly desperate, he twisted on the seat and looked at the pointing carbines, at the hotly malevolent eyes. Conant's hand crept toward his holster.

"No, no!" Vada cried out. "Dad — Banjo! Don't let them kill you! Don't die because of me! It won't help!"

Don Ricardo snapped a word quickly to his men, who were on the point of triggering. They reluctantly held their fire, muttering, frowning. "Good advice!" he complimented the girl, and smiled again, showing a flash of white teeth.

For a moment he considered her where she sat in the buckboard. His dark eyes kindled with a bright inspiration, founded upon virility and a connoisseur's taste in responsive feminine intimacies.

"Do you mean," he asked her, "that to save their lives you would be willing to go with me? Well — perhaps not willingly, but obediently, at least." He waited, and said, "If not, they die! In either case, of course, I take you with me."

"I —" She choked up, before whispering, "I'll go with you."

"You promise to obey me in every way?" he demanded.

She shuddered, avoiding Banjo's tortured eyes. "Yes."

"Ah!" he murmured caressingly. "You will help to console me for the loss of the money, *amada mia!* With your lovely hair and your . . . Ah, in Mexico I will be envied by all men who see you!"

An involuntary sob broke from the girl, at which the don looked affronted. "No sadness, now! I forbid it! No regrets. You would have wasted your charms on that lowly, impoverished cowman? I shall teach you a higher discrimination, a joyous appreciation of Don Ricardo de Risa — me!" The brag was spoken only partly in jest, for in his boundless masculine vanity he believed himself to be irresistible to women. As generally he was when he put himself to it.

"Hombres, rope those two gringos on horses and send them off!" he ordered.

"Alive, by virtue of my charitable nature, which I doubt they appreciate. Instead of gratitude, they glare red-eyed murder at me! *Bien, bien,*" he sighed ironically, "we cannot please everybody. Tie them good and tight! I do not want them sharpshooting on my trail. Gringos are so persistent. So damned singleminded."

To Bishop, he commented, "You are very quiet, Rogue!"

Bishop nodded his head slightly, his hard face blank of any expression, deep-set gray eyes masked, opaque as marble. "I'm thinking."

"Suspiciously quiet!" The bone-handled guns in Don Ricardo's hands hadn't wavered for an instant. "I distrust you most when you are silent! Nor do I want *you* sharpshooting on my trail — you, the most damned persistent of all! I do not like that look in your eyes! I do not like your thoughts, whatever they may be!"

"I'm thinking," Bishop said, "that you've dropped down a few notches from what you once were — from the man you were in the old days when we first met. Remember those days, Rico? Not that you were ever any shining angel, no more than me. Plunder, sure, and you never had the morals of a tomcat where women are concerned. But we — us of the old bunch — did have a kind of code then."

The don's face darkened. "Then? Not now?"

"Not now. Not you, anyway! We wouldn't have done what you're doing. Tie up two men in their saddles and turn them adrift to starve or die of thirst? Carry off a young girl, tender, innocent, to . . ." Bishop paused.

The opaqueness dropped from his eyes, unmasking a baleful anger of such glinting intensity that the don stepped back a half pace. The *guerreros* scowled fiercely, yet halted their advance with ropes on Conant and Ballinger.

"I'm thinking," Bishop said with biting distinctiveness, "what a son-of-a-bitch you are!"

16

He was taking a desperate risk. Ordinarily, the epithet could stand as an admission of defeat, a curse at the winner, shrugged off by the winner. In the tone he delivered it, though, it was much more: an intolerable insult.

He pushed it further. "Don't ever again mention your highborn background or any of that Spanish *aristo* crap! Not to me! It would turn my stomach! To me, right this minute, you're nothing but a —"

"Stop!" Don Ricardo hissed, making the word sound oddly like *esstop* in border *pachuco* vernacular. "Stop it, Rogue!"

He wasn't alluding to the scathing invective. Not entirely, though it played a heavy part. He had detected ominous signs: the look in Bishop's eyes; a tensing, barely perceptible, of a tendon at the root of Bishop's right thumb — preliminary to a fast gun-draw.

"No! No, Rogue! I'll kill you!"

He didn't want to kill the big gringo. Life wouldn't be the same without him. They had gone through so much together in the past, sometimes paired, more often clashing in conflict. The existence of each other gave spice to their lives.

"Sure you'll kill me, Rico! You've got all the advantage!" Bishop jibed him. "Guns out, cocked and lined at me. Trigger 'em, if that's your style now! But the second shot — mine — will drop you for keeps! You know it, gunman!"

Don Ricardo lowered his guns. "I am not a gunman!" he objected, his pride stung. "A gunfighter, yes. Like you."

"Prove it!" Bishop challenged. "Holster your guns, stand off, and draw at your pleasure. I'll be ready for you," he said, and immediately regretted tacking on that short sentence, a betraying slip of the tongue.

After briefly considering the proposition, or pretending to, the don wagged his head, smiling knowingly, realizing at last that the insults were purposely intended to goad him into committing an angry error — a rash act that would cut down his present advantage. Give Bishop an opportunity to flash out his guns, he'd swiftly turn the tables and dominate the situation.

"You're ready, Rogue, yes! Ready to put the drop on me while I holster and stand off, eh?"

He had no illusions that he could safely outmatch Bishop in a straight draw. The shade of difference, one way or the other, was too slight to offer survival to either one of them. He entertained a grudging but well-founded respect for Bishop's wits and explosive potentialities.

"No, *amigo!* Nothing doing! I am running this game, not you. My orders stand. Conant and Ballinger may go, tied securely to horses, pointed north. The girl goes south with me. The money is lost, but I refuse to quit empty-handed!"

"You're a sour loser, Rico."

"A hard loser," the don corrected. "So are you, hell knows! Which brings up the question of how to stop you from trailing me to Mexico."

"I'm wondering about that," Bishop said.

The pair of bone-handled guns tipped up again, lined at him. "There is a simple answer!"

"Simple?" With slow deliberation, Bishop brushed open his black coat, exposing two shell-studded gun belts, two black butts protruding from trimmed and laced-down holsters. He knew to a fraction how far he could test his old adversary's readiness to fire point blank at him. "Not so simple — unless you give your crew the nod to blast me at the same time! As I guess you will, if your guts can take it," he said.

The don's eyes clouded. His anger had dissipated, leaving him in cold-nerved control of himself. "If I must, I must," he countered dispassionately, forefingers tightening firmly on his triggers. "Self-preservation . . . For that motive, friend has killed friend, brother has killed brother. Law of the jungle. We live by it, Rogue. And die by it. Survival —"

"Cut the philosophy! On my last breath, I'll drop you!"

"I know you're hard to kill. But it seems the only answer. Do you have a better one?" A cynically crooked smile accompanied the query. "I'm sure you do, and it would give me no benefit! I'm like a woodsman who has caught a large panther by the tail, you know?"

"I've been called a lobo. Not to my face."

"Panther or lobo, turn its tail loose and it will pounce on me! The solution to the problem is obvious, yes?"

Bishop nodded, conceding the validity of the analogy. Freed from the aimed guns and carbines, he would certainly prowl on the trail of Don Ricardo de Risa, track him down, pounce on him, settle the score for this bit of business. The don was perfectly correct about that, knowing him.

He looked at the tear-streaked face of Vada Conant, crying quietly in the buckboard. She was so young, full of spirit, easily hurt. In the ordinary course of events, he supposed, she'd be destined to become a happy bride, wife, contented mother, a matron caring for her household.

Well, perhaps there was merit in living a safe and settled life. Possibly satisfaction, a sense of fulfillment. He had never tried it, but he held a tolerant view of it. His own rootless ways, suited to him, weren't recommended to everybody. Temperaments differed. It took all kinds . . .

"Goddam it!" he swore under his breath, looking once more at the crying girl. If it weren't for her . . .

His large tolerance didn't cover the corrupt ruining of her life, as long as he had any means of preventing the tragedy. To let it happen would invite bad memories. Getting himself out of this deadlock with the don wasn't enough.

Aloud, he said, "Yeah, I think I've got a better answer." Then louder, for the benefit of the *guerreros:* "The money!" They pressed forward, listening hungrily, disregarding a warning gesture from their leader.

"You are raising false hopes, Rogue! You can't possibly know where Doc Sunday hid the money!"

"I might. A few minutes in the brush, and I'll know for sure."

"A shallow trick for you to make a brush fight!"

"I'll leave my horse with you," Bishop said. Slowly, he unbuckled his gun belts and let them fall to the ground. "There! I'm unarmed and afoot." He raised his eyebrows to the *guerreros.* "How strange it is for Don Ricardo de Risa to reject forty thousand dollars!" he remarked to them in Spanish. "How improvident! A share of the money is yours, no?"

They chattered vociferously at Don Ricardo, who, giving way, snapped at Bishop, "Two of them will walk behind you, to make sure!" He had never before seen the notorious gunfighter unarmed, but still he deeply distrusted him from sore experience.

"Make sure of what? A bullet in my back?" Bishop shook his head. "I go alone, or I don't move from here! I'm gunless, horseless —"

"And tricky as Satan!"

He shrugged. "We both play a tough game. Before I hand you the money — if I find it — I demand —"

"Demand?"

"Right! I demand we make a sworn bargain. You'll give me the girl, free and clear, for the money. Your solemn oath, in the hearing of these caballeros."

The ragtag ruffians straightened up, appreciating the compliment. Caballeros, them. Why not? From all accounts, those old-time soldiers of fortune, the Spanish conquistadores, had sought mainly gold, too. Gentlemen adventurers.

"Give the man your oath, *jefe!*" they clamored. "We want the money!"

The don uttered a harsh laugh. "I predict you will go on wanting the money! He can't produce it!"

"Behold, our *jefe* becomes a prophet!" jeered the oldest one of them. "Or could it be that the gringa girl has fired his blood so hot —"

"Silence! You are impertinent, Tolo!"

"I am forthright," retorted the oldster. "A sensible man, I say, does not lose a fortune to win a woman!" It brought growls of agreement. He paused and went on. "Only a fool gringo would do that! Or perhaps an *aristo* like you. As for us, we are down-to-earth sensible men." He motioned with his chin at Bishop. "And as the big gringo says truly, a share of the money is ours."

"But I tell you he can't . . ." Don Ricardo broke off, knowing how useless it was to try changing their stubborn minds. They were men of action, not of thought.

The money meant as much to him as it did to them, but they had got the mistaken idea that he placed a higher value on the girl — because of his objection to Bishop's proposition. He couldn't get across to them his firm belief that Bishop had some trick up his sleeve. They were dazzled by hope.

"Very well, then," he told Bishop. "My sworn oath. Why you insist on it I don't know, for I hardly expect you to come back — certainly not with the money! I suppose it is part of your play to get yourself out of a very bad spot, yes?"

"You've got my guns and my horse," Bishop reminded him.

"Part of your play! You know I wouldn't agree to let you ride off with your guns! So you sacrifice them for your life. *Bien, bien!* This is an occasion to remember."

"I'll be back," Bishop said. "Give you my word."

"You do? H'm." The don stroked his narrow mustache, a sign that he was puzzled. "Honest word?"

"Bedrock guarantee."

"Return emptyhanded, my men will go berserk!"

Bishop nodded. "Reckon so. I won't be gone long, I think. Wait here for me, and don't do anything yet to Conant and Ballinger, eh?"

"I'll give you a few minutes, that's all. We have already wasted too much time here. Go!" The don watched the tall figure stride off. "Go to the devil!" he muttered irritably.

It was more than a few minutes before Bishop broke out of the brush and paced back to the road, where he found Don Ricardo engaged in an argument with his men. The don wanted to push on south forthwith, contending that Bishop had simply pulled a bluff and done a disappearing act. The *guerreros* mulishly shook their heads, although they obviously were having misgivings. Conant and Banjo stood silent, and Vada sat forlornly in the buckboard.

They all looked at Bishop, with varying emotions ranging from incredulity to flickering hope. The dispute hung suspended. Conant, the first to notice the black leather satchel Bishop carried, asked bitterly, "Is that all you went for? Doc Sunday's old veterinary bag?"

"That's all," Bishop replied. "Doc slung it at my head, driving down to the Pueblo ruin. Missed, and it fell in the brush. That was his real purpose, though it didn't occur to me at the time. The brush made a hiding place for it in a pinch, as long as he marked the spot in his mind."

He raised the old satchel. "This," he said, "is what brought Doc out alone tonight, looking for it. But we came along before he could search. He didn't even have time to hide his horse. Finding he was here — that was when I put two and two together. I remembered this spot."

Don Ricardo paced slowly forward like a bristling terrier on tiptoe, old Tolo and the others scuffing behind him. "A vet's bag!" he spat. He eyed it with stony disgust. "Is this a joke or have you gone crazy?"

"I get it!" Conant exclaimed. "Sure! Doc Sunday always kept his black bag with him. It was like a part of him. He wasn't ever without it."

"Except when he threw it at me," Bishop said. "He couldn't risk carrying it along to de Risa's bandit camp in the Pueblo ruin. You can guess why."

"You bet I can! He'd crammed the money

into it. Most likely he used his bag many a time for toting loot. A handy cache, never out of his sight, nobody giving it a thought. I'll be damned!"

"You will be damned, I promise, if this is what I think it is!" stated Don Ricardo. "A piece of humbug!"

"Want to open the bag, Rico?" Bishop offered him.

He stepped back, bumping into a man behind him. "Open it yourself! I wouldn't trust you not to have a bomb planted in there, or a nest of rattlesnakes! You were gone a long time."

"Had to search. Found it caught in some mesquite." Bishop pressed the brass catch and opened the bag. He dipped his hand into it, his fingers creating a crisp rustling that brought gleams to the eyes of the *guerreros.*

"If this isn't good American money, then I've been poor all my life," he observed. He picked out a crisp banknote, fluttered it, let it float to the ground. "The bag's full to the top. Look!"

Don Ricardo looked, and caught his breath at the sight. The faces behind him were suddenly leaner, sharper. Old Tolo reached a sinewy arm past him, fingers hooked. He drove an elbow at the old ruffian and found his voice, whispering urgently to Bishop, "Close it, quick! They grow crazed! Give it to me!"

Bishop snapped it shut, but drew it back. The faces became more starkly menacing. The carbines came up, pointing at him, and harsh breathing hissed like strong wind through cracked shutters. He knew it was touch and go for the next few seconds.

"This is yours," he said. "This wealth is yours." He let that sink in. "First there is an agreement to keep. A sworn oath. *No es verdad, caballeros?*"

The harsh breathing slackened. The carbines gradually lowered. *"Es verdad!"* grunted old Tolo. He snatched up the fallen banknote. "Give to the gringo what is his, *mi jefe.* He has brought back the money!"

The others concurred, one of them saying, "Settle the bargain quickly and let us be on our way! It is unlucky to break a sworn oath, even to a gringo!"

"I am a man of my word!" declared the don grandly, holding out his hands for the bag.

Bishop held onto it. "You're several other things I could mention, too. What do I get out of this?"

"You get your guns, your horse, and the girl. I throw in the buckboard as a favor."

The don beamed. "A token of our friend-ship!"

"No share of the money?"

"None. Winner takes all, Rogue! I am the winner."

Bishop eyed him with severe disfavor. "Goddam shark! Banjo," he called, "get the buckboard turned round, and head north. Climb on, Conant. Don't take forever!"

He picked up his gun belts. Strapping them on, the bag between his feet, he growled bad-temperedly at the closely hovering *guerreros,* "Give me room! Banjo, you set? Then what the hell are you waiting for? Get going!"

Don Ricardo sighed pensively, watching the buckboard depart. "It grieves me to lose that girl! So lovely. So young and fresh. So —"

"Quit drooling, you've won the cash, blast you! You can buy half a dozen females!"

"Not like her! I have discrimination, high standards in femininity. My taste —"

"Ah, shut up!" Bishop tossed the black bag to him. He mounted his horse. The buckboard had got well away with its pas-sengers — Vada and Banjo and Conant, and two saddled horses tied behind. "So long, thief!"

"Do you plan to track after me, Rogue?

For this money? For revenge?"

"No, Rico. A bargain's a bargain."

"Adios, amigo!" cried Don Ricardo, happily hugging the precious bag. "May the gods grant me more such victories as this!"

"The gods," Bishop said, heeling his big black horse, "might just do that."

He caught up with the buckboard where it had halted at the turn-off branch that led toward the long Amarillo road. A road southeast into Texas, which for personal reasons Bishop didn't care to revisit for a while.

Tom Conant sat on a rock beside the road, at a distance from the buckboard, studying his boots, looking lonely and out of things. What Banjo Ballinger was saying to Vada could be heard, for his voice carried in the still air of the coming dawn. The eastern sky was graying. At sunup a slow breeze would sweep over the land, soon die, and the heat of the day would set in with the blazing sun.

"Honey, I'm dead broke. My herd's scattered like feathers in a gale. I'm wanted by the law for shooting up that town, stealing a train, wrecking it, then breaking out of jail! Shoosh! I can't ask you to marry me."

"You haven't. I asked you."

Conant looked up at Bishop, then down again at his boots. "That's how it is. Busted cowman. She loves him. Well, better a poor man's wife than no wife at all. She'll win him round." He paused somberly. "God help 'em!" he said. "I won't be running for re-election for town marshal, that's sure. I'm busted, too." And in his eyes lurked a frantic fear for his invalid wife.

"You're not cut out for a town marshal, anyway," said Bishop bluntly. "Get back into cattle. Make a fresh start."

"Easier said than done, at my age."

Bishop moved on. He had a vigorous man's impatient attitude toward an older man's anxious worry for the future. Whatever the future might hold, he was arrogantly confident that he'd make do to meet it. Conant got up and trudged after him tiredly, shoulders sagged.

Dismounting at the buckboard, Bishop stood frowningly pondering. His mind went off at a tangent, harking back to the past, to the days when a few bedrock principles ruled conduct as a matter of course. From that standpoint he took a brief view of himself. He had accused Don Ricardo de Risa of selling his tattered honor and going all bad. Yet here he was, himself, weighing self-interest against self-respect.

It wouldn't do. "Here's the bill of sale on your beef herd. Doc Sunday canceled it, which turns the herd back to you." He gave it to Banjo. "After Conant gets his wound patched up, you better have him hire a crew of riders to round up those cows. He can handle the sale for you, too, on commission as your agent. Meantime, you mosey on back home to Arizona. You and Vada."

Conant perked up tremendously. "I can do it, Banjo! Cattle's my natural trade." He hesitated, before asking wistfully, "Would there be a place for me and my wife on your Arizona spread?"

"You bet!" Banjo responded. "We could work together. But we're forgetting one thing. The cows are scattered miles everywhere. Running a roundup crew — spare horses, couple of wagons, grub, all that — costs money!"

Bishop checked a sigh. That, too. Well, it had to be done, damn it. "The money's on tap," he said. "More than enough. A lot more."

He began producing sheafs of banknotes from the inside pockets of his coat, from under his shirt, and even from beneath his hat. Piling them on the ground, he commented, "Good thing it was dark back there, or Rico might've noticed I seemed to have put on some weight! Conant, count out twenty thousand dollars of this for Banjo. What's left is mine."

They stared in amazement at him and the hoard, Conant blurting, "Didn't you hand it to de Risa?"

"He thought I did. He's in for a surprise. What he's carrying in that black bag is Doc Sunday's kit of veterinary tools at the bottom, stuffed under dead-dry leaves, with a layer of money spread on top — three or four thousand dollars. Maybe enough for Rico to pay his *guerreros.* That expense can come out of my cut."

"Man, you took an awful chance, pulling a switch on *him!*" Conant rolled his eyes. "And you unarmed then! If he'd dug into the bag —"

"Rico's sharp," Bishop conceded. "I had to play it sharper, each move. Now get to the counting, will you?"

Banjo, recovering from his speechless shock, raised an uncertain objection based on a pinpoint of conscientiousness. "Wait a minute, let me think. I recover my beef herd. That is, I get back the bill of sale, anyway. You skinned de Risa out of the cash price — or most of it — that Doc Sunday paid me and then stole back. I mean, de Risa stole it for Doc, and Doc double-crossed de Risa. In any case . . ."

Vada kept nudging him to drop it. Being a woman, she was more realistic, less inclined to dispute fortune. Banjo looked at her and then at the money, his objection wavering. "The question is, what right have I got to part of it, and how much, if any?"

"I don't have a head for figures," Bishop lied. He could calculate to a fraction the percentages in poker. "We made a deal. It stands, regardless of, h'm, details. Consider your share as damages paid for all the grief Doc Sunday brought on you. The wear and tear has been pretty hard."

Banjo started to mention that much of his bodily wear and tear had been caused by Bishop's roughshod tactics, but Vada put in sensibly, "Besides, Doc paid the money to you in the first place, for your herd. A straight business transaction on your part."

"Good girl!" Bishop approved.

"In fact," she pursued, "all the money is actually yours, Banjo."

"H'm!" grunted Bishop, not caring for that line of logic. "Let's get our business transacted here and go our ways. After Rico digs into that bag, he and his *guerreros* are likely to come hot on my trail. Hurry, Conant! Give it to her, not him. She's his manager."

215

He gathered up his share of the money, stuffing it into his pockets. Vada watched him severely, like a wife who felt that her husband had been outbargained. Banjo and Conant made vague, embarrassed sounds of gratitude to him. Bishop mounted his horse and gave them one stiff nod of farewell.

Riding off, southwest bound, he muttered with wry humor to himself, "Would have served Rico right if I'd let him take her!"

ABOUT THE AUTHOR

L(eonard) L(ondon) Foreman was born in London, England in 1901. He served in the British army during the Great War, prior to his emigration to the United States. He became an itinerant, holding a series of odd jobs in the western States as he traveled. He began his writing career by introducing his most widely known and best-loved character, Preacher Devlin, in "Noose Fodder" in *Western Aces* (12/34), a pulp magazine. Throughout the mid thirties, this character, a combination gunfighter, gambler, and philosopher, appeared regularly in *Western Aces*. Near the end of the decade, Foreman's Western stories began appearing in Street & Smith's *Western Story Magazine,* where the pay was better. Foreman's first Western novels began appearing in the 1940s, largely historical Westerns such as *Don Desperado* (1941) and *The Renegade* (1942). The *New York Herald Tribune* reviewer commented on *Don Desperado* that "admirers of the late beloved Dane Coolidge better take a look at this. It has that same all-wool-and-a-yard-wide quality." Foreman continued to write prolifically for the magazine market as long as it lasted, before specializing exclusively for the book trade with one of his finest novels, *Arrow in the Dust* (1954) which was filmed under this title the same year. Two years earlier *The Renegade* was filmed as *The Savage* (Paramount, 1952), the two are among several films based on his work. Foreman's last years were spent living in the state of Oregon. Perhaps his most popular character after Preacher Devlin was Rogue Bishop, appearing in a series of novels published by Doubleday in the 1960s. George Walsh, writing in *Twentieth Century Western Writers,* said of Foreman: "His novels have a sense of authority because he does not deal in simple characters or simple answers." In fact, most of his fiction is not centered on a confrontation between good and evil, but rather on his characters and the changes they undergo. His female characters, above all, are memorably drawn and central to his stories.